Praise for *SHADE AND BREEZE*

'A magic voice. Working with the coming-of-age in a small-town narrative, Quynh Tran creates a world completely of its own kind, a story of belonging and estrangement, and of the refugee experience. In a sensual, dreamy prose, still so very real, with an authority reminiscent of Ocean Vuong's *On Earth We're Briefly Gorgeous*, Tran has written a first novel that shines like a precious gem.'
— Monika Fagerholm, author of *Who Killed Bambi?*

'A perceptive debut, where the significant events are intentionally placed in the background, in line with the family's wishes. Not everything should be discussed, claims the mother whose anger instead turns into a physical condition – a slap here and there. Nobody is capable of seeing how their actions cause a ripple effect, how human darkness is passed down through generations. In different ways, the family members try to find a mutual place where they can love one another. This makes *Shade and Breeze* a complex, delicate, and wistful debut. It deserves to be pulled into the light.'
— *Sydsvenskan*

'With great sensitivity to detail and tight, charged language, Quynh Tran tells of the family bond as strength and shackle, and of the emigrant's eternal homelessness.'
— *Vi Läser*

'Quynh Tran writes beautiful, saturated prose.'
— *Expressen*

'Quynh Tran's prose is vivid and cinematic, sensuous and full of images and descriptions that are both suggestive and alluring… An elegant and impressive debut.'
— Svenska Yle Literature Prize Jury

SHADE AND BREEZE
Quynh Tran

Translated from the Swedish
by Kira Josefsson

Lolli Editions
London

NO THANKS, BYE

For weeks, she had warned me: one morning I'd have to go out with her. All I had to do, and all I had to remember, was to look pitiful.

So we practised.

Do it... Look pitiful.

Eyes focused, lips looser. Neither pouting nor taut.

Yeah, like that.

Má giggled. I held this look, directed my gaze to where the wallpaper met the floor, and let it linger there. Then I traced the skirting board around the corner and into the kitchen. An unhurried, slack gaze.

One morning she woke me by stroking my temples and eyelids. Hieu was still in his bed, which was across from mine. We snuck out. It was too early, and Má and I were on our way out.

Early spring. Pale, pink sun.

The supermarket had just opened and the regulars were already stationed at the slot machines. Má asked to speak to the manager. We were given the supervisor. She asked if Má knew Finnish.

We went to the slaughterhouse. The shift manager asked if Má was strong.

We went to the town centre. Má wanted to try the flower shop even though she knew nothing about flowers. We stopped at the first traffic light, just a stone's throw from the centre of town. A glimpse of the school building's yellow stucco. We were about to cross the street when she remembered. School was starting. She looked at her wristwatch.

Goodbye, my pearl.

That's what she said.

I set off to join the children in the schoolyard – ours was the most magnificent school in town – as Má turned around, heading back home.

The next morning, she woke me at the same early hour and we went straight to the flower shop. A humid place, with the windows all fogged up. We were received by an elderly lady who was more than happy to phone her manager. Since we were her first visitors, she said. I looked at the flowers (begonia, geranium, coneflower) while the lady described Má to her boss: 'Friendly, cute... Oh, what else can I say... cute.' She ended the call and turned to us. She had good news, she could hardly contain herself.

'Magnus might be able to offer an internship—'

Má interrupted her mid-sentence. 'Internship. No thanks, bye' she said, and we went for the door.

'Internship.'

'No thanks.'

'Goodbye.'

Odd Swedish.

I turned to wave at the lady, but she had already turned her back to us, now bent over an enormous pile of mulch that was trickling down towards her feet like brown water. Her entire being was soft and indolent.

When Má woke me up next morning I had an impossible urge: I was sick of her, I almost wanted to spit in her glum face. We went to the laundromat, it was right around the corner.

She got the job.

She was to work every weekend, Friday to Sunday, afternoon to evening. Starting in June. 'That's very good,' she said, 'my language classes end in May.'

I sprinted all the way to school.

In the afternoon, when I came home, she was standing in the doorway between the kitchen and hall, as if she'd been waiting for me. She told me that my presence hadn't been necessary, I had simply served as additional insurance, she would have landed the job regardless. She told me she didn't even really want it. I asked her why, and she said it was because so many Vietnamese worked there.

Early afternoon. Hieu was sitting by the kitchen window. Little sweat stains on his shirt. He was resting his elbows on the tabletop as though to cool down.

DETOUR

On weekends, when everyone was home, I sometimes woke to the sound of softly falling rain. Hieu's crumpled sheets across the room. I would close my eyes and fall back asleep. A day that had long since begun. The rain's increasingly faint thrumming on the tin roof, the rain's cold on the windowpanes, as though the windows were my own skin.

Late-morning sounds from the living room. They were eating out there. I pictured the scene, how they ate and watched TV – walked to the kitchen, back to the living room, onto the balcony to gaze down on the wet spring street, all soft and shiny with rain and traffic; then to the kitchen; then back to the television, always with full mouths, chewing. The balcony door left ajar. A slow, docile breeze.

The gulls had hushed, the cars had left the car park. A night that had spilled over. I got up, joined them. Muted light. Tennis on the TV. The food lukewarm in glass bowls.

A few evenings I followed an urge to walk to the housing expo, where I sat down on a bench and gazed out over the water. Older couples exercising together skirted the bay, which was almost entirely ice-free. Brief, friendly glances. Dog owners with their dogs, intermittently stopping. Dogs that didn't know each other approached with jerky movements until they were face to face, frozen, hesitant; tense, sand-coloured dog bodies in the milky light of streetlamps, motionless save the spasmodically opening and closing nostrils.

The wind was picking up. People abandoned their balconies,

shut the doors. Treetops grew murky against the sky.

Instead of taking the shortest way home, which was through the neighbourhood with the old wooden houses, I chose a detour. I crossed the car park of the shopping centre. A lone woman was standing by the traffic lights. She was clutching a paper bag and bending now over the gulls that flocked around her. She smiled. The smallest chicks were hopping in place. Their eyes were fixed on the woman's hand as it reached into the bag. And when fluffy pieces of bread flew over their heads, their caws echoed over the street and created an odd harmony with the rumbling of idling cars in the car park behind the centre.

Sometimes Hieu was home when I came back. When that was the case, I would always kick my shoes off, loudly.

SALARY ADVANCE

Friday afternoons Hieu would come home with drumsticks marinated in milk and honey. He roasted them in the oven. Drawn by the sweet scent, I impatiently climbed on the kitchen chairs. I crouched or kneeled in front of the oven to watch the transformation through the green-glossy window: the chicken's sticky outer layer hardening, caramelising.

We often ate without her.

Sometimes she came home late. Hieu would boil water and then we'd gather in the kitchen, each with a cup of tea. We sat quietly as she stirred chicken into the sticky rice, letting fat and colours meld before the first bite.

Poor children... Same food every day... What a mess...

Then she'd disappear into the bathroom.

She had already described to us long ago how the kitchen uniforms smelled. They arrived at the laundromat in droves and from a distance looked like glaciers rising inside the tall wire carts. Kitchen uniforms that, when unfolded, were sticky all over with oil-stained sleeves and the linings brown with dirt. A sharp smell which, once ingrained, was impossible to remove. She'd done her best to avoid it, to not let the grime touch her skin.

Her white work smock had its own hook in the hall. We'd inspected it in detail on her first day; we turned the sleeves inside out, checked behind the buttons, peered inside the enormous pockets. Everything was white, even the seams were white, and there was that bitter, citrussy scent.

Both of us were wondering, each on our own – though it

did come up in conversation, Má and the laundromat — what sorts of things were happening there. She started to work overtime a lot.

Hieu and I took to sitting together, in front of the TV and around the kitchen table, out on the balcony. We pondered various questions: what kind of detergent did they use, did they wear plastic gloves, and if they didn't, wouldn't Má's hands get scorched; did they sit or stand while sorting the laundry and what about the heat, the heat from the irons, from the machines, the aggregates, her shiny face and the smell she said stuck to her arms and legs like a film, the smell that didn't go away no matter how many times you showered. What did her boss look like, and that work smock, how could it smell like that hanging on the hook in the hall?

When she came home we stopped talking. We fell silent, as if reverent before this new kind of fragility in her. Her new, nervous laughter.

One night Hieu plucked up his courage. In a quaking voice he asked if we might be able to visit the laundromat someday. It was so close, after all. The question made her roll her eyes. She scoffed, she laughed. Under no circumstances would we be invited.

Má was paid at the end of every month. Sometimes, like when we bought the red plastic chairs for the kitchen, she asked for a salary advance.

FOTO ELITE

Hieu's books were scattered all over the apartment. I never saw him read, but the books always looked well-thumbed. He did what some people do with books: scraped them, smelled them.

I flipped through his books when I was home alone. It was in *Literary History* (all-white cover), in the margin above a photograph of Hagar Olsson, that I first came across *Isabella*. Carefully printed in fine pencil; straight lines and judiciously proportioned curves per the general rules of handwriting. That is to say: written with great care.

On every page in the religion book (bright red cover): *Isabella* in block script, *Isabella* in cursive, and after less than a hundred pages: *Isabella* in capitals, *Isabella* in red and purple, in blue and orange, *Isabella* in graphic, multi-dimensional script, swelling past its outlines, onto the text and illustrations of the final days of Jesus.

The spring term ended with a ceremony. The school gym was crammed with students, family, staff, and kids from other schools. Cheek by jowl. Palms burning, an unbearable excitement. One by one we stepped into the light. Now and then, not often but still more than once, a murmur rose from the audience. Family and friends clapped the hardest and took the most photographs. Má had brought her camera, too. A new camera; the night before she'd sat down with the device and its instruction booklet in her lap. In the kitchen, all night.

It was Hieu's last year at Lagmans. I was graduating from second grade, he sixth. It was tradition that the outgoing class would put the cap on the event. Their mouths: *oh oh oh*, a delicious accent, their singing grew in intensity, voices intermingling. The final note had not yet faded before the room erupted in cheers, ending the evening's programme. The entire room whistled and stomped in honour of Hieu and his large, proud mouth.

Afterwards, waiting for the bus: she hung our blazers over her arm. The evening sun was pressing on, pushing against the eyes. The bus arrived, bursting with people. I fumbled with my card. The driver looked at me, looked at his wristwatch, then looked at me, looked at his wristwatch... Má and Hieu set their sights on two seats in the far back and the door closed, cutting off the queue that slithered down the street. I took a seat in the front, the only free spot left. My dress shirt clung to my skin.

The A/C on at full speed. The driver, now in a good mood, relaxed.

Outside the bird cherry was in full bloom. Gravel smattered against the metal framing the windows. To my left: the love birds in the form next to mine, Milla and Taisto, embracing.

I looked back, Má already had her eyes on me, miming *almost there* while pointing at the digital display. Hieu was snuggled up underneath her arm, the one she wasn't using to point. Somehow our blazers covered his torso fully so that only his head was visible. Her arm slithered under his chin, it looked like she was cupping her hand over one of his ears. She was resting her head on top of his and his eyes were closed, his head wreathed.

The bus emptied out. We stepped into the humid air. Hot asphalt, silhouetted high-rises. Má and Hieu keenly trudged up the hill.

This was the summer I came to master the Cruyff turn. The secret was simple: if you do it merely to humiliate your opponent it doesn't matter how excellent your performance is; it's a superfluous skill. A talent that doesn't benefit the team is useless. Herein was the move's central aspect, which I understood early on. Repetition was necessary to master dribbling, so I practised. Má practiced photography. She sat with her instruction manuals, baring her top row of teeth, licking her lower lip. She was going to drop off her first rolls at Foto Elite, in the centre of town.

RED EYES

Má and I were each in a corner of the sofa. Hieu was in his room. Má was watching TV. Three stacks of photographs on the table, most of them rejects, all-black or depicting some kind of round, ambiguous light, a lamp or a moon.

Some showed the rooms of the apartment: the kitchen, the living room, Má's bedroom, mine and Hieu's bedroom, the bathroom. Blurry close-ups: the phone, the kitchen faucet, the desk. None of the photos of Hieu and me showed our eyes, just our backs, cheekbones, scalps.

A close-up of the schoolyard swings. Flower bouquets and white shirts. These were from the end of the term ceremony.

I kept looking through the stack.

Photographs taken inside the gym hall, from the ceremony. A girl stepping onto the stage with her classmates. That same girl – blurry, in motion – on her way off the stage. In the final picture she's about to sit down on her chair in the audience. She's looking straight at the camera.

I spent a long time with that photo.

Half-lit: suits, dresses, young children's blurry movements. The girl is looking at the camera, her arms are by her sides, she's completely at ease. In the background, Hieu and his silly smile, stock-still in the bustle behind the girl and her red eyes.

Má looked up from her corner of the sofa.

That's Isabella... She looked so pretty.

It was the first evening with the photographs. Hieu came out and joined us on the sofa. He started to flip through one of the stacks, we both did; he sat next to me and I watched him systematically look at the photographs, one by one, an equal amount of time dedicated to each of them.

It was only later, when we were in bed, that I realised he'd brought one of them to the bedroom. He was looking at it when Má came in. She opened the door and went straight for his bed, where he lay half-covered by the sheets, on his belly, propped up on his elbows with his chin resting on his hands, the photo placed on the pillow in front of him. Má entered without a word, took the photo, and left without a word. In the muted light of his bedside lamp I was able to glimpse that last picture of Isabella, with Hieu smiling in the background. The only picture that showed both of them.

I would go through that stack of photographs many times. Finally they were all scrambled and I would guess at the chronology – dates, hours – and organise them accordingly. I also tried organising them according to other principles: colour, light, focus. Finally I organised them by the size of the girl's eyes: largest eyes first, smallest last. I had no time for the other pictures.

In order to understand the correct order of the photographs, I would have needed to understand what preceded them; to know something about Hieu's interior life, what occupied him during those months. Which is to say: a big love, blossoming red, spilling over the edges.

THE ARCHIPELAGO, OUTDOOR RECREATION

People often said that ours was a small town. A nice little summer town. Great summers: the archipelago, outdoor recreation.

Now and then Má would take us to the indoor pool for the day. Temperate, quiet mornings. The lady in the reception seemed surprised, almost offended, when we showed up.

The pool was deserted, not a soul in sight aside from the lifeguard who padded back and forth with a folded newspaper in hand, sometimes looking up to check on us. Hieu and I walked between the pools until we finally, shivering, got into the kid's pool. Hieu flopped around so much that water splashed out. The lifeguard appeared unbothered. Hieu swam several laps, back and forth, without resting. Finally we got out and joined Má in the hot tub. She brushed the hair from our foreheads.

Later on we were standing outside the lobby waiting for Má to blow-dry her hair in the women's changing rooms. It was a gorgeous day. Pleasant breeze, the treetops quivering. Má came out and photographed us standing on the warm steps.

On our way home we visited the ice cream shop on the square. Vanilla cones in hand, we went to sit on one of the benches by the tall doors of City Hall, from where we had a view of young families wandering between the flowerbeds. Hieu's hair, the sun glimmering in it. He was restlessly bouncing his leg, one foot tapping the ground like a tense coil, it kept going for a long time until Má noticed and put a hand on his knee. He stopped, and she kept her hand there.

Cars crawled forward with their windows down. Drivers and passengers in sunglasses. Families on their way to the beach, energised and joyous, a summer town.

We crossed the square, walking homeward. Má paused, the camera like a stone pendant around her neck.

MAGGIE & TONY

For weeks Hieu had walked past the movie theatre, looking at the poster in the window: a woman in a red velvet dress and black earrings, a man in a dark suit, eyes closed, head in her lap. A love story from Hong Kong. He waited until the final day of its run: a matinée, half-price.

Má had never been to the movies, not since we got here.

It was beach weather, sunny and cool, we were wearing light clothes. By the time we arrived the other moviegoers had already entered and taken their seats.

It was almost full. Buttons were opened and there were chocolate bars, pistachios. Rustling wrappers.

Hieu spoke the film's title.

He had been talking about it for weeks.

Someone falls in love with someone… Two couples move into the same building simultaneously and become neighbours. Soon, the woman in one of the couples and the man in the other begin to suspect that their respective partners are having an affair. Their suspicion turns into an obsession and they start enacting the events they imagine.

Má snuck out during the previews, stooping in the darkness. She came back with a big bottle of soda, chips, popcorn.

The first scene shows the two couples moving into their respective rooms. The movers carry the furniture up the narrow stone staircase. Everyone is trying to squeeze past each other. Everyone is sweating, except for Maggie and Tony. Maggie and Tony: the woman in the first couple, the man in the second couple. Maggie & Tony: the couple on the poster.

The landlady: *What a coincidence! Moving in the same day!*
Tony: *You can put the chair in the corner.*
Mover: *You have a lot of stuff for a couple!*
Maggie: *Mind that mirror, mind how you hang the mirror, it's fragile!*
Tony: *Are these magazines yours?*
Maggie: *Yes, they are my husband's.*

The second scene takes place in the drawing room. A group of people, among them the landlady, are playing mah-jong around a round table. Everyone is dressed to the nines. Among them: Maggie's husband, facing away from the door. Maggie enters the room as Tony leaves it – their eyes meet. Maggie goes to sit with her husband, who briefly touches her arm before returning his attention to the mah-jong tiles.

Má got up and left again, without explanation.

Everyone lingered for the credits. The lights came on and we found ourselves in the midst of the crowd streaming toward the exits. The other visitors were excitedly discussing the film and other topics, talking while looking straight ahead at their gesticulating hands. It was funny the way they signalled while talking.

Outside, the talk stopped. Everyone fell silent, squinting at the clouds. A heavy rain. One after another, the moviegoers made a dash for the car park. Then a string of solitary, creeping cars, inexplicably slow traffic. Má in the far distance, across the road, under the awnings outside the pharmacy. She had let her hair down – we'd soon be back home again – and it was slicked against her face. She would spend all night in bed as warmth spread under the covers.

Hieu took my hand, pulled me along, guided us across.

Má was looking straight ahead. Her clothes smooth and cold against her body. The gleam of cars in the store window, Má's eyes. The sewers gushing. She said something inaudible.

On the whole, it was a rainy summer.

EVERY SINGLE ONE OF THEM

Low fog outside the classroom window. I reunited with my classmates, home from their holidays abroad. Thin white shirts over their red, sunburned skin. On the first day we were asked to write about our summer holiday, with the promise that anyone who so desired could share their account at the end of the period.

I had to recollect a time scarcely distinct from the present. It was still summer. We were freckled and rosy, now back in the blinding glare of overhead lights.

Summer holiday...

The clouds, and then the sun.

The times when it rained, and the times when the wind was blowing.

The teacher got up and left. My classmates fidgeted at their desks. We had been left to our own devices. And now, at the sight of my classmates – freckled, rosy, with pale hair, with dark hair – I blinked, and was subsequently overwhelmed by an odd sense of vertigo, a flash of vertigo that somehow cleared my mind.

I pictured an uninterrupted sequence of days: the wind, the light, falling asleep and waking up, the afternoons, the nighttime rain.

Then I started writing – you could say I was writing like a beast.

Josefine had written about her family holiday in India.

It was hot in India.

Like a sauna.

They went to the market.

They bought spices.

They brought these spices home with them.

Unfortunately, she apologised, she hadn't had time to write more, but the teacher said thank you, that was great.

Emilia had written about her stay at a riding camp in eastern Finland... A terrible story, which she, moreover, read inexplicably slowly. Nevertheless, the teacher claimed it was excellent.

And on it went.

I was able to pretend that my decision was spur of the moment, that my choice to share was some kind of impulse, so when everyone who had said they wanted to read had done so I raised my hand, and even though it was now technically breaktime – running in the hallways, fun and games in the schoolyard – the teacher had no choice. I straightened my back and began to read.

The beach. The waves and the sun.

My story was about when Má took us to the beach.

We weren't at the pool; this took place in Fäboda. We swam in the sea, where the waves salted our lips. We ate ice cream on the beach and when darkness fell we took the bus back home.

I heard my voice, I felt my rapid pulse and sped up my reading. I had written sentences, with commas and adjectives. My grammar was impeccable. I read with pathos.

The burning sun.

The tall waves.

I described the bus ride and the way Má struggled to blow-dry her damp hair once we arrived back home.

When I was done, the teacher looked at the white clock over the classroom door. He looked at us, praising each one of us, thanking us for reading so beautifully. Five minutes remained of breaktime. A strange atmosphere. He looked us over, but did not give me a glance.

Me and Matti, the teacher. The whirring of the fluorescent lights.

It was difficult to focus for the rest of the day. I was raving in class, I was loud, I was pushed by something unknown, a newly awakened appetite.

Impeccable grammar.

Matti must have been shocked by my reading, must have been taken by surprise.

Tuomas had described several weeks spent helping his brother tinker with his moped. Jürgen had written about the Kokkola Cup, the football tournament, it was all about football, he accounted for the results, who scored the goals, which teams won the medals, on and on; that was it...

Josefine... Siri... Emilia... Timo... Tove... Jürgen... Every single one of them... Terrible...

Breaktime was different. Besnik and Juri and I were teammates. Before the final period of the day, in the late afternoon, we made a new discovery. Our movements were suddenly synchronised. It was new, and it wasn't a coincidence, because we did it again and it worked, and the next morning we did it again and it worked again. It was about getting the ball back as soon as we had lost it, and we had to do it in concert, instantly: we rushed the opponent with all our might and if the ball was passed back we pressed on, together, like a swarm, until we recovered it. It was simple. Our classmates stood by, arms hanging, confounded, and let us take the ball as if that was what was expected of them.

This worked for weeks, until some of the older students came to stand in the way, protected the ball, just stood there, and we crashed into their massive frames.

Besnik and Juri and I: for a few weeks we were one single, irrepressible organism; a storming, laughing cluster.

It was a time of games, of play.

TAMPERE

We were going to visit Tampere for autumn half term, Má and me. She had been able to borrow a car from a co-worker. We left early on a Friday. She woke me at dawn. Hieu was breathing deeply, rhythmically across the room. It was to be his first weekend alone; for weeks she'd talked about it.

Má had been talking, always in the kitchen, and we had listened: *Nothing to worry about, just a weekend, no big deal.* Hieu would then straighten his neck as his gaze found its way out across the yard, all the way to the lindens by the road where passing cars could be heard though they were nearly indiscernible through the foliage. It was new, this way he sat with his back straight – his torso one with the backrest – and whenever we were at the kitchen table and Má assured us that everything was going to be alright, he gazed farther and farther out, his attention in the far distance, on the fields and trees, his face absolutely still, not blinking, not even his mouth moved.

At dawn, in the car park: Má glancing at our bedroom window one last time. Then she started the engine and we crawled out of the car park, down the block, toward the motorway.

I had consulted an atlas. In the middle of the line that bisected the map between Jakobstad and Helsinki: Tampere.

Má's co-worker's Ford Focus. We carved our way into the country, bit by bit. That's how I thought of it.

I slid back and forth in the back seat: to the left to look at oncoming traffic, to the right to look at the strange, soupy landscape. The seat cover was soft and cool against my arms.

Má turned up the volume. It was the first real day of autumn. Rusty colours welled forth. I leaned my face against the window. Trinh Cong Son sang about unhappy love:

like the waves long to caress the beach
I find my way to your warm embrace

I woke up to Má's unexpectedly bright, quick voice. The sun was up. Dust lay still in the air. Laughter everywhere.

The cars were neatly parked along the low fence outside the house. Bushes with red and black berries were in the yard. We'd barely got out of our car – there was still a chugging sound under the bonnet – when a man and a woman, the hosts, came running to embrace us. Mrs Ngoc and Mr Chim, constant smiles, teeth always visible. Mrs Ngoc in a long, turquoise dress, Mr Chim in a button-up shirt and a pair of round glasses attached to a string. Now and then he took them off and glanced briefly at the glass before returning them to their place at the tip of his nose. Má spoke excitedly about the drive as they brought our bags in.

We crossed the lawn. A red wooden building with a flat roof. A short-haired woman was in lively conversation with a man on the terrace. The man smiled and nodded at us, asking if Auntie Tei Tei wasn't coming too, and Má replied that it didn't work out this time, of course you could never know with aunt Tei Tei.

Mrs Ngoc gave us a tour of the house. Light feet over the creaking floor: *bathroom, sauna* – her turquoise sleeves hung in the air – *and this is the guestroom, as you might recall. . .*

We entered a tidy kitchen with a glass door and a small

window facing the backyard. The backyard, the bank of the ditch, the forest clearing. That's where they were slinking around, the hosts' kids, two siblings. Má pushed me further into the room, not towards the door but straight at the window, as if she hoped that her light touch on my shoulder blades would cause me to lift and float through the glass – and then I glided across the smooth, dew-glossed lawn of our hosts to join the playing siblings. Behind me I heard Mrs Ngoc's voice, going the opposite direction and already remote. *I'll just tidy up a bit, then we can start.*

The siblings were shouting in invitation to join them. They sprinted in between the tall, sparse trees, Thu followed by her younger brother Xuan. At one point Xuan turned around to make sure I was following them, he turned one single time, mid-leap, and looked at me with his green eyes. Green eyes. The shade of jade jewellery.

It turned into a vivacious day. The siblings were enormously excited. They took me to the boulder: a massive, moss-clad boulder which rose as if out of nowhere in the midst of the greenery, gnarled with rough edges on the sides and smooth on top. We climbed up, which gave us a view of the gravel road and the rye field that reached all the way to the town's grey buildings. Then we stretched out on our backs and read comics. City traffic rumbled in the far distance like low, protracted howls.

It was cloudy, not particularly warm, but when the motorway maintenance workers turned up and started their screeching machines, asphalt fumes blurred the colours and transformed the warning signs, the uniforms, and the branches of the trees into one single jumble. I began to laugh.

I couldn't control myself. I climbed down and ran all the way back to the house, sped into the siblings' bedroom where I changed into my new cotton shorts and ran back to the boulder. We stayed there, reading, until late at night. The workers left. It wasn't until Mrs Ngoc called us in for dinner that I understood what I'd witnessed during that short time when I changed my clothes.

They were sitting around the round table in the salon. Má brought a cigarette to her mouth. There she was, cards in hand. Troubled face, her frown as she took a first drag, her gaze; everyone focused on the patterned plastic cards. The radio was on, the television was on, but everything was silent. At the centre of the table: a sloppily constructed pile of banknotes in varying colours. Má played alone, Mrs Ngoc and Mr Chim played together, Mr Tèo played alone, and there was the woman who'd greeted us on the terrace earlier, the younger woman in sunglasses I thought I knew but would only recognise the following day as Lan Pham.

The game's objective was to combine thirteen cards in three different ways – made up of five, five, and three cards each – in accordance with the principles of poker. In the end, everyone showed their hand to determine that round's loser and winner. Over and over again. Sometimes Mrs Ngoc and Mr Chim would take turns to get a bit of rest. The others played through the night.

Green eyes! They were what I saw in my mind's eye as I curled up on the mattress in the siblings' bedroom, on the floor next to their bunk bed, trying to fall asleep to the sounds on the other side of the wall: chairs scraping against the floor, the kettle, sharp whispers.

After a morning outside with the siblings – we ran across the almost finished asphalt, over to the rye field – I joined Má. She was holding her cards in one hand and caressed my hair with the other until she found her solution: she broke her full hand, making it a partial straight, sacrificing high pairs for colour. To the right of us, by the window, was Lan Pham with her round glasses and short, lank hair. It really was her. Her cards were easy, not necessarily good, but at least they didn't require difficult decisions. She balanced restlessly on her tipped-back chair as she waited for the others, looking out over the yard and the car park. It was as if she was already anticipating her next smoke break, when she could put her heart-shaped red sunglasses back on again. It was the very first thing she would do, even before exiting the house.

Mr Tèo was sitting across the table from us. I noticed his hand movements: the gesticulating, bony fingers in constant flow, hands like jellyfish underwater. And then he was ready with his cards. I looked at his fleshy lips, they spread as he talked, they took over his face and sort of replaced it, became his entire face. He was talking about Japan. Japanese film. One of his tirades.

Mr Chim took off his glasses. He cleared his throat, an almost inaudible sigh, then put them back on again and turned his attention back to the cards that Mrs Ngoc, his partner in the game and in life, held between them. They'd won several rounds in sequence now. And they were about to win again; somehow that was evident from the silence that had settled over the table. In the midst of all this Má noticed the mosquito bites on my legs. She opened her eyes wide, a horrified expression. I moved my hands over the fresh swellings, red and oblong; smooth, throbbing bubbles.

Our final night in Tampere. I snuck into the bathroom and turned on the shower, letting water run from the small of my back to my feet, where I had scratched the skin raw in several places. I stood there a long time, letting my legs go numb before I turned the water off, dried myself, and snuck back into bed. I heard a whisper from Xuan in the bunk bed. He went to the kitchen and returned with four ice cubes. We sat down on the mattress on the floor and Xuan let an ice cube melt over the bumps on his neck. I inched closer to him and placed an ice cube on his forehead. He jerked, then closed the eyes and smiled. His face was still, only the mouth was moving.

That's when I saw Má, standing in the crack of the open door, hands hanging in front of her... As if she'd frozen mid-movement.

She appeared a moment later with an aloe salve that she squeezed onto my skin, straight from the tube. With long strokes she rubbed it into my legs and my arms and my hands, followed by my neck, the front of my neck, until I turned my face to hers and closed my eyes. When she kept going I turned on my side, demonstrative, eyes still closed. She left the salve by the mattress and quietly got up and left the room.

The siblings' breathing: uniform rhythms, entwined.

Soft laughter, clinking tableware. They were toasting out there.

In the car going home: grey clouds compressed in the grey sky. Má glanced over her shoulder, looked at me. Her hair was gathered in a loose bun. Her gaze: something glassy and immeasurable, her face blank, a shiny membrane reaching the hairline. She was talking to me, she was trying: she wondered if I thought Hieu had seen any girls while we were away. Maybe that girl Isabella. Or someone else... He was that age, she said, you could see it on him. I looked out the window and wished that all that was to come would pass me by.

The others had been in cahoots, they had cheated, she claimed, *conspired*. She scoffed, everything she said was preceded by a scoff. She raised her voice, only to immediately, before the end of the sentence, lower it again. She scoffed and jerked her head back, it was as though she found the whole thing silly, and before I could say anything she asked if I thought these people would ever leave anything up to chance, if I thought it was a game for them. She took her hand from the gear and fumbled in her pocket for a pack of cigarettes. It was strange that Mr Tèo and Lan Pham could stay sharp, she said. Fine, young people don't need sleep, but how was Mr Tèo able to play at that level for so long, she couldn't help but find it strange, *odd*. It would be naive to think anything else, she said. Then there was silence.

Through the window I watched the clouds disperse and join again like a dirty, elastic clay. She rolled down the window and let in the humid air. In her left hand, between pointer finger and middle finger, she held a cigarette. She brought it to her mouth and took a drag, then switched to a tweezer grip – cigarette between top of thumb and pointer finger, with the remaining fingers spread in a feather-like arch. I pictured Má at the card table, sunk in the deep silence of one of the rounds: she turned to Mr Tèo to respond to something he'd asked her earlier that night, a question about whether she liked her job – a short, simple question – and she'd begun to orate about tensides that reduce the water's surface tension so that the clothes can be properly cleaned, and deeply so, the mutual trust among the co-workers, their generous boss who had agreed to replace the ventilation system if each of them worked overtime for two hours – two hours! an entire ventilation system! – and the fresh air that resulted, *like night and day*. She went on: You might think that perfumes made from essential oils – lavender, orange blossom, so-called natural perfumes – would be preferable to artificial ones, but no, under no circumstances would they get her to agree with that. She took every chance she got to employ the classic detergent, made with an artificially produced lemon fragrance – why would she choose something else? In the lab you have full control: potency, nuance, notes; the classic detergent was a classic for a reason, something the majority of customers agreed with. *But...* she said... *To answer your question... I really do enjoy working there, it feels like my competence is valued, you know?* The game had paused, it was a rare event, all eyes on her, even Lan Pham had straightened her back and was now leaning forward on her chair with an interested expression. Má moved an extinguished cigarette to her mouth. The tweezer grip. She placed the cigarette in the corner of her mouth, where it hung off to the side. She lit it. The flame brought out the shade of her lipstick and with it, the hint of a grin.

She changed her grip one last time: the hand's five fingers like a bird's beak facing the mouth. The final drag. In her cupped hand, a soft glow, soon to be tossed into the thick air where it would vanish, bouncing soundlessly on the asphalt.

CHEWING

Was he asleep or pretending to be asleep when we set off, whispering and in a hurry? A soft wind outside. That's how it must have started: a soft, buzzing wind, the sound of whistling from the yard, and he must have sat down at the kitchen table, gazed out over the field, trying to recall Má's comforting words.

We came home on Sunday, late, just before the night was at its darkest. We walked in without a word, simply showed up, and the first thing she did was open the fridge. She was so horrified that, for one brief moment, she buried her face in her hands. Then she pulled the balcony door open and found him, her firstborn, sitting out there bare-chested, hands in his shorts pockets and feet on the railing. Before he could even look up, she pounced, delivering a slap on each cheek, one single fluid motion. His stone face in the dim light. He didn't move, he gave her no reaction, she went back inside.

He took his feet down and stood up next to me. We looked at the silent street. The lamps on the building next door illuminated the neatly parked bikes. I stared at his hands. It was like I was frozen in place. He gripped the iron railing, which was dimpled by paint, as if he were on a ship.

She'd asked him: why hadn't he eaten, and why was there sand on the floor, *by the bed, your bed, why is it all sandy?*

The following afternoon Má stood in front of the open fridge, which was full of ready-made pizzas and milk and Karelian pierogies and fruits and vegetables she'd got for him to eat while we were away in Tampere. Hieu and I were at the kitchen table, him listening to music on his headphones, me doing my homework. The scent of ginger and garlic. Má with the apron on. She broke down the wet lettuce in the frying pan. A sizzling sound; Hieu looked at the stove, turned down the volume of his music. She tossed in a handful of bean sprouts and red bell pepper. Tofu, sesame oil.

Hieu took off the headphones.

We served ourselves from the frying pans, where the food crackled and steamed in front of us. We slurped, our faces disappearing into the bowls.

After two servings Má leaned back and gave a loud moan, like a complaint, and we laughed raucously. *I can't eat another bite* she said, and then she put out a plate with sliced beef tomatoes sprinkled with salt and pepper. It was the nicest meal we had all year. Hieu was wearing a light-grey velvet button-up. The marks on his cheeks had almost faded, leaving just a lingering blush.

MR TÈO'S TIRADE

Imagine if we'd established our civilisations independent of each other, meaning East and West, separate... I mean, just consider... We could have had our own expertise in physics, chemistry, biology; we could have had our own industries, our own technology, everything could have been made for us. For example, just think: if everything was made for us, do you really think we'd be sitting here in this light? I mean, just look! I can see all your pores. Is that what you want, was that something you considered when you purchased this lamp, that it would make all your pores visible? Just kidding... But think of it for a second, entertain the idea. Think of the art, the paintings – think of the films! Have you ever noticed how different Japanese films are from American and French films, or German for that matter, and I'm not just talking about the way they're written or the way the actors talk and move... I'm thinking, above all, about the lighting... And the colours... Have you ever considered what it would look like if the cameras and the film and the chemicals used in post-production, all these things... What would it have been like if they'd been made for the way we look and move? Of course I'm talking about the Japanese now, saying 'we'... Well... Imagine if we'd invented the radio, if it had been us optimising recording technology. What would Vietnamese folk music have sounded like then? Different, no doubt, better suited to our voices, our music... In any case... There's no difference between us and the Japanese anyway, in terms of genetics, DNA, that's what I'm saying, we share almost exactly the same DNA, or at least we're more like the Japanese than the Westerners... Especially the Finns... What do we have in common with them? 'You Asians,' that's what they say... 'Vietnamese,' he said... Someone at my internship... He said, you Vietnamese, he said we're hardworking, that we work well, he said the Finns are known for the same thing... They're hardworking he said... And I nodded: 'yes, yes,' 'sure, sure'... I could barely keep a straight face... And guess why... I'm sure you want to know why... Well, let me tell you... This same guy, the week before, just a few days prior, had gone to the shift leader to complain about being made to work on his lunch break! Are you hearing this? He wanted to sit in a room and eat his food and do nothing else, maybe he'd talk to his colleagues; are you getting this? This guy, who couldn't even put together a fixture and eat his sandwich at the same time, he... You must excuse me... What a bloody... Finns... Hardworking people... This guy, I swear... Well, no, but I've been thinking a lot about light and shadows recently – okay, I see you laughing and by all means, but let me explain, how can I put it... Alright, so Westerners, one thing that distinguishes them from us is that they tend to like things that are superficial, clear... And here I'm talking about both objects and spaces... Yes, spaces... While we prefer depth, shade... I've been thinking a lot about the way they build their houses here... Where to start... Even a thing like the roofs, the way they construct them, compared to Japanese buildings... In Asia the roofs are made large and wide like parasols, so that shade falls over a larger area... And Westerners, on the other hand... Take your roof for instance, the roof under which we are currently seated – of course it protects against rain, inclement weather, and so on... But the shade! No shade to speak of! On the contrary, they seek to let in as much light as possible... Unbearable... Yes, we all feel that way, everyone around this table feels that way, because we're Vietnamese and we understand the mystique of shadows, of course that's what they say, they like to talk about... What's that thing they call it, 'Oriental mystique', and I suppose that's what they mean by it... Our appreciation for shadows... We're likely to lose that appreciation too, though... We've become so accustomed to electric light that soon enough I imagine we won't even notice it... In the end I suppose it's not all that bad... Just a question of aesthetics... But the thing that really gets my goat... Really, the thing that makes me actually angry... is their tendency to keep the lights on when they're not needed, even when it's harmful! This summer I went to a few cafés, and, well, you all remember what the summer was like... All everyone could think of was cooling off... And no matter how hot it was inside, these white people insisted on keeping those lightbulbs on... And nobody complained! They just sat there! 'Nice, nice!' It makes me furious... I should stop... It makes me so angry... But listen... What do you think they do at that point, when it's too hot and all the lights in the building are on? Well, I'll tell you: they turn on the fans! First they chase out all the shadows, then they turn on their whirring fans! White people! Crossing the river for water! Oh, well... I shouldn't let myself get so worked up... Next time I'll speak up... No, but really, I will...

ALL THE BUTTONS

That autumn I studied with the efficiency of a god. In the lead-up to a test I was in the habit of reading until I could account for the central details from memory, something that usually required hours of repetition. This fall it was as if I'd been endowed with superpowers. I skimmed the readings, swiftly but attentively, and when I quizzed myself by closing my eyes first and then looking at the text, knowledge came to me in steady streams.

I was sitting by the living room window.

Hieu was never at home. He was in junior high now, and his days were long.

I watched people move from the car park to the buildings, and walking the opposite direction, on the narrow pavements up the hill and away from the neighbourhood, toward the motorway, the city bus.

I studied.

A mother with a child in one hand and a pram in the other was standing by the gooseberry bush outside the kiosk. They moved slowly, paused at the next bush. The eager hands of the child, his big eyes looking at the thorns and berries. The sturdy metal benches in the kiosk's dining area, an arm's length from the cars that crept by. A lone woman was eating a sandwich on one of those benches. Two boys, each with an ice cream cone. Gulls.

Hieu entered the apartment with a bunch of government envelopes in hand. He asked for Má and my reply was prompt: she might be in the grocery store. He left, took the lift down, the door left open. What was he wearing? Shorts and slides...

In the car park, the afternoon rush. An entire family was now eating in the kiosk's seating area. Reggae music came through an open window somewhere.

The door to the bathroom flew open. Má came out wrapped in a towel. She brushed her hair in front of the hall mirror; wet shiny hair over her shoulder blades.

I was doing my homework.

Hieu was on the road outside the window. Something was up with the way he moved, as if he wanted to run but was somehow prevented, so that he sort of skipped forward instead, disoriented, as if the street he'd walked down so many times before had suddenly become foreign to him.

I rested my hands on the open book. I watched him stand on the street and look around. He entered the kiosk.

He exited the kiosk.

He kept walking down the pavement, clumsily and according to his own strange rhythm. He stopped in front of an elderly couple, got right in front of them. They ignored him, stepped to the side and continued on their way. When he crossed the street and went into the little pharmacy, I closed my eyes and pictured him in there.

Hieu: Excuse me.
Pharmacist: Yes?
Hieu (panting): Have you seen Mum? I'm looking for my mum.
Pharmacist (kindly): No... I don't think so.

He came out of the pharmacy. He walked homeward, in our

direction, but turned abruptly and walked up the hill towards the bus stop. Clutching the stack of mail in his hand. Má came up behind me with her hairbrush. She laughed in surprise.

Is that Hieu? Is he wearing slides?

I turned the page in my geography book.

When he finally came home Má was sautéing vegetables at such high heat that I had to stand in the doorway to hear them.

The electricity bill, the electricity bill is here, we've received the electricity bill.

Má now dressed, Hieu in slides.

I often looked at him after this. He wore hoodies, flannel shirts. One evening, on my way home after late practice, I glimpsed him outside a grill, in the middle of a crowd, everyone in big trousers. Hands in his pockets, he was leaning against an illuminated window. I sped up, and once I was home I couldn't keep myself from telling Má.

His shirt was entirely unbuttoned... But not the top, the top button, that one was closed...

Má took her time. She raised her eyebrows and stared at the ceiling.

Get on your bike and go there at once, tell him to button his shirt, all the way.

She said it in one flowing sentence. Not with her regular voice, but still it was a voice I recognised, with her eyes in the ceiling, as though she, too, had been talking to somebody else.

I biked off, still wearing my football kit. It had got cold. I locked my bike to a pole by the canal and walked to the town centre. On the crest of the hill I crept forward. Commercial jingles played from the stores on the esplanade – *price cut*, *exclusive offer, edullinen tarjous* – and shadowy figures with slumped shoulders everywhere you looked. I found him almost exactly where I'd seen him before. This time he was leaning against a different store window, still with his shirt oddly buttoned. A few people in the group shook hands with the others and left. I saw him: his eyes and his distinct smile beneath a streetlight. He was in the middle of a discussion, gesticulating, his gaze darting in every direction. I turned around, hurried back to my bike, and then, on my way home, all the way home, I tried to forget it: the top button closed... a good look...

IT WAS STILL DAWN

The minute I came home after school I went straight to the living room and spent the rest of the afternoon there, engrossed in my schoolbooks. These days of rapidly falling darkness when everything else was out of play. Seagulls circling, the final rays of the afternoon sun a brief lustre on the eyelids.

The canals that connected Euphrates with Tigris.

Glacial erosion, wind erosion.

Pine, spruce, birch.

Aspen, grey alder, rowan, pussy willow.

Oak, linden, maple, wych elm, white elm, ash, hazel.

I studied and they fell silent, lingered in the doorway, hapless like two ghosts watching me excel in complete self-control. To truly study — it wasn't something Má and Hieu could ever understand. We had written about our summer holidays, I had shared with my classmates, Matti had been absolutely stunned. I had shocked him.

Back straight, stately. Books piled on the windowsill.

A back straight like a rod. An inexplicable lightness.

I went to our room, to the far end of it, near Hieu's bed by the window. I got a knit sweater out of the closet and on my way out of the room I slipped it over my head. I left the door open at an angle that would allow Hieu to observe me from behind where I sat in the living room, absentmindedly pushing the hair from my face. Now and then I sat up even taller. The delicate joints of the fingers. Upper arms, neck, the nerves of the back, everything had to be softened in one single motion. He couldn't bear it. I knew he was watching me from inside the bedroom.

Days of absolute commitment.

Yes: I studied like a god.

But there was one Saturday, an ordinary day, when the apartment was empty. Doors wide open. A looming, enigmatic absence. They must have gone out. Their first excursion, I pictured it, bright and easy.

I imagined them in the still, dark morning. Alone at last. Groves of iridescent blueberry shrubs shining in red.

The beach was somewhere. Má held his hand all the way there. Her other hand: the rolling bag – Má's black suitcase with the combination lock – arm kept tense, ready to parry any slippery effects of the gravel. They'd already arrived. Across the street people came out of their cars, opened and closed the doors, looked around distractedly. Hieu was wearing his crinkly jacket. Dawn still, and he still wished:

There, no, not there... there... THERE, no, NOT there... NO! THERE, THERE, there...

It was still dawn and they were drifting, aimless. It's how I pictured them on the beach: unsystematic.

They sat down on the sand. The cold, smooth beach and the autumnal wind.

Swooping gulls by the shoreline.

It was still dawn, it was dawn until it turned grey, and he would look for what had surrounded her but was now gone: a lazy cloud, the flickering foliage down the slope, the strand of hair that tugged towards the centre of the face. Sharp bones behind her cheeks, prominent in the grey light. She opened the suitcase on the sand. Baguettes with salted pork rolled in tinfoil. The thermos filled with tea. The circulars.

Cars. Blueberry shrubs burned by frost.

They were out all afternoon. All afternoon: the neighbourhood was so quiet. I pictured Má and Hieu down at the beach and I was unable to read, I felt blood pulsing at my temples, I sat on the chair with my arms hanging straight down.

They went around the corner to the sports field, where kids ran, indefatigably, from dusk to dawn. Má and Hieu, leaning against the fence to the tracks, children turning to face the sun, baring their teeth to it.

The evening came into focus. They would walk home on the tree-lined avenue. A sharp image. The asphalt lit up. His overgrown boy's body in front of the rolling bag. They could have moved unobstructed in a straight line but didn't know that the evening market closed at exactly this hour, and that people, for a short time, would stream in every direction and force them to forge their path in a crisscross pattern. He pointed at the food stands under the parasols. They stopped and looked. The oil splattering on the plastic windowpanes; the wheat dough hard, white, but supple; the powdered sugar a glassy, alien substance. Oil fizzled and the sounds started all over again: the cawing of birds, soft teenage shoes on the asphalt.

I pictured Má and Hieu squinting in the bright light.

She'd woken him early. That must have been how she did it, one of those early fall days when darkness fell fast; she woke him, a finger over her lips. It was early, it was still dawn when they ventured out.

Afterwards: Má went into the bathroom. She ran the water and stayed in there for a long while, singing in front of the mirror, by the sink. Outside we listened to the TV, which was on. Two brothers and the TV on. Her cloth slippers swept over the tiles. We kept listening.

Then she sat down at her vanity, bedroom door cracked open. There was something relentless about her. She began to put on her face. I went to stand in the doorway, as if to say something to her, but I stood there silently, wordlessly taking in the smells. I went back and she came after me. She bent over us.

She took us in her arms.

She went out.

We kept watching, surveying.

The door slammed shut. The sound of her heels in the hallway, going down the stairs, crossing the yard. Hieu sprung up, eager, a transformation of some kind. He went in the direction of the bathroom and filled his lungs, exposed his teeth, yearning like a dog.

Outside: a very sharp wind. The motionless, lively body under the covers, as if waiting for a command, ready to be put in motion.

This dog-like aspect of him would keep me up at night. He lay sleeping in his bed across the room, he was almost naked. He'd had the top button closed, his vest stuffed in his jeans, the jeans so large you could barely see the shoes. I thought about Isabella, how he must have looked at her, his desirous puppy dog eyes across the school cafeteria.

It was during these sleepless nights that the crisp, almost crystalline, images came to me for the first time.

I remembered the period when we'd just arrived in Jakobstad.

Gunnel.

Gunnel, full of care and initiative.

Gunnel standing in our stairway on Christmas Eve, hollow-eyed after her long shifts at the hospital. Má and

Gunnel, on Christmas Eve, in the apartment door, where they exchanged bouquets of flowers while Hieu and I received a box each of chocolate pralines. It was how they kept in touch nowadays. Gunnel would pinch my cheek. Then she hugged Má and Hieu. First Má: a long, quiet embrace. Before they let go of each other Gunnel would sweep her hand up along Má's back, on to her neck, hold her head in her open hand. Then: Hieu's head in Gunnel's hand, his hair falling over the back of the hand like tassels on a lamp.

Images of Gunnel.

The first days with Gunnel.

The photograph shows us lined up in the vestibule of the airport, a whole group of Vietnamese. Children and adults, visibly cold but happy: squinting, grimacing, thumbs-up, fifteen to twenty of us in jackets that are too big and have strange logotypes. Má is holding me in her arms, Hieu next to her, close. Among us too, the Finns, thumbs in the air. Open mouths. Remarkably enthused faces.

I found the photograph at the back of a drawer in Má's bedside table. I had to sit with it for a long time. The first scene: arrival. The snow. Gunnel at the airport in Oravais. Gunnel who hugged each and every one of the arrivals, including the adults, as though we were her own children. Gunnel. That cheerful stranger who talked to everyone though nobody could understand her. The wind that howled against the large airport windows.

We introduced ourselves, one at a time. Gunnel came close, she smiled her warmest smile, and then it was as though she had a realisation, because she jumped and began to rub the outside of her arms while looking at us all. We were made to follow her through the length of the illuminated arrival hall, she walked in front of us and gestured with the length of her arm as if to say come, come. It was an important day in our lives. For Gunnel it was perhaps the most important.

It must have been that way.

In the photograph she's wearing a knitted hat, which droops over her rectangular glasses. Her arms: a little blurry, a hint of movement, perhaps restlessness? She is, as they say, on the go.

We were introduced to Lan Pham. There she was all of a sudden, in all her splendour, Lan Pham who spoke Vietnamese and Swedish. She was the link between us and our new home. Lan Pham with the strong jawline. We flocked around her. Our first questions concerned this strange lady. Who was she? Why was she so generous? *Gunnel*, Lan Pham responded. *Sponsor family. She is going to help you integrate into this society. She and six others.*

Má would come to speak of her even after that first period, even much later. Gunnel, an unusual figure, *sweet* but *so difficult*. It was as though Má was making sure we wouldn't forget her.

These were the images on my mind. Gunnel and the snow. Hieu and Isabella.

EUROSPORT

Late that autumn Hieu brought a friend home. Má, from inside the bedroom:

Is that you, Hieu?

They moved with ease and confidence. Hieu's white shirt collar lay pressed underneath the sweater.

I brought someone.

The girl's back floated into the kitchen and they started to whisper behind the closed door. The sound of boiling water, the lid of the rust-yellow tin coming off. The scent of jasmine. He was making tea for her and they were giggling.

The home was tidy. Shoes neatly lined up in the hall.

There was ski jumping on Eurosport. The jumpers' uniforms fluttered as they sailed forth. Helmets, protective glasses.

'Kazuyoshi Funaki… known for his enterprising V-style, where he leans forward at an extreme angle, parallel to the skis—'

He glided down the steep ramp.

'We'll see if he can control his nerves on home ground—'

At the jump he straightened his body, then hovered straight, unmoving in the air.

'Graceful—'

The dial indicated 90km/h.

'Very elegant, and oh my, this is a long jump—'

'And there… We're seeing Funaki landing, Funaki has landed! Did he just take the gold? We'll know shortly, but first here's the replay, notice the slightly shaky landing, though that fades in importance when we know that the jump measures 132.5 meters! 20 points from every judge! There's no doubt, Funaki takes the gold...'

Má came out in a bathrobe, her hair in a tight bun. I told her a Japanese jumper had won. She looked at the TV.

They're so skinny... They look like ghosts.

She went into her bedroom without closing the door.

Up Close With Nature on Swedish Channel Two.

'In our midst... What you'll see now is footage of a lynx in Västmanland, watchfully and soundlessly sneaking up on a vole.' The only sound is from the birds: cheep, cheep chip cheep chip cheep cheep cheep cheepchipcheepcheepcheepcheepcheep. The lynx is crouching in the tall grass. It gets up slowly, gaze trained on the prey. A rustling. The lynx freezes, paw in the air, hesitant. Clipped, swift, almost spastic movements. The long back leg that drops, lifts, stops in the air. Cheepcheep cheepcheepcheepcheepcheepcheep cheep cheep cheep. The lynx leaps in the direction of the camera and disappears from the frame. Cheep cheep cheep cheep cheep cheep. A few humming bees. The vole is neither heard nor seen.

Má came out with her face made up. Eye shadow, pastel lipstick. She glanced at the kitchen, then the TV. She tied her shoelaces.

On Eurosport: tennis in Tokyo, Martina Hingis playing Steffi Graf.

I heard Má stop behind me. I turned around and there she was, in the hall, her half-open purse hanging from her shoulder. She looked up, straightened her back.

You've been watching TV all day.

She walked out into the hallway, the door was wide-open,

she'd called the lift and now she was waiting. She was waiting, and I followed her as though pulled by a rope. A sudden urgency. I stepped into my shoes and trailed her into the stairwell. Very softly I shut the door to the apartment.

Footsteps. You could already hear Hieu and the girl moving inside. The television still on, the tennis; the long duels between Hingis and Graf, the grunt that followed each stroke. But mostly giggles, Hieu and the girl giggling brightly, Hieu's giggle and the girl's giggle, one and the same loose, airy giggle. They were heading to the hall. Maybe they were going to look at the photographs on the wall.

Má held the lift door open. Her brushed hair lay straight and shiny over her shoulders, the sunglasses were loose in her breast pocket. She held the door with about as much impatience as you can hold a lift door. We went down, the lift creaking. I looked at our reflection. Then, out of nowhere, Má asked if I was the one who had tidied the apartment. It was cloudy outside. Teens were running from the street to the houses. People were getting bags and boxes from their cars. It was dinnertime and we were walking to the city. Má put on her sunglasses and gazed at the grey sky. As soon as I glanced at her she looked back and I wondered what she was thinking, if she was thinking what I was thinking. Hieu and the girl had probably been in all the rooms by now. What was he showing her? What was there to show?

We set out for the shopping centre. The sky was thin; at any moment now the cloud cover would break open and let through the real light.

In the grocery store we walked past the produce, the home electronics, and the clothes; past the seafood, the bread. Our destination was the deli and the grilled chicken. Má pointed at one with particularly dark skin.

We sat down on a bench outside the entrance, with a view of the enormous car park. A blurry crowd in the dusk. Má opened the bag; steam billowed out. She placed the golden chicken, which was swollen like a pincushion, between us. Grease came oozing out. Má ploughed her fingers into the rounded breast and brought a thick piece of meat to her mouth. She chewed with her mouth open – it was warm out – while simultaneously, moving fast, as if someone was egging her on, pulling off one of the thighs and handing it to me. People were walking in and out of the shopping mall and we licked our fingers.

The convulsing movements of the clouds. They remained in the sky all evening, twitching.

We walked home in silence. Má was in a hurry, she dragged me behind her, sometimes it was as though she was about to tell me something, you could see it on her lips, the way they quivered, she inhaled as though preparing for a performance, but she didn't say a word, not even in the lift going up to the apartment.

The girl had left. Hieu was sitting on the sofa flipping through the circular and Má went straight for it.

You cleaned, huh? Good!
She saw me play basketball. Then she wrote me a note.
And?
Yeah, she wrote to me.
And then what?
Yeah, and then I wrote back.

Má gave him a long look. A confused expression: she raised her eyebrows and squinted.

Afterwards, when we'd gone to bed and I was sure that even Má was asleep I snuck out of the room. I turned on the lights. The shoes were still neatly lined up in the hall, the trash cans were empty, everything was in its place – the newspapers and the banknotes on the shelf, the clothes in the closet, the shampoo bottles along the wall of the shower. He really had tidied the apartment. Suffusing the space, the distinct scent of pine soap. He must have done it when we were sleeping. I turned off the light in the kitchen. In the sink, the teapot and the sieve with swollen tea leaves and jasmine flowers.

Má had asked and Hieu had responded. Her name was Laura. She had Finnish parents. She had red hair and lived in Pörkenäs, by the sea, across town, far from the centre. This was not Isabella. It was Laura.

COBRA

When Má came home from the laundromat she would make a big pot of soup that she put in the fridge after Hieu and I were already in bed. Certain nights, when I couldn't fall asleep, I would soothe myself by listening to how quiet she was. How long could she take to turn the key, to open and close the door, to not wake us? How quietly could she rinse and chop a leek?

One night I had the idea of surprising her. I lay in wait for a long while and as soon as I heard the lift I got out of bed and went to stand on the threshold to the kitchen. Nobody else entered the building at this hour, I knew it was her. I was going to astonish her.

Afterwards, when I'd gone back to bed, there was something else there too. My longing had to share space with something new, and this new thing excited me.

She'd arrived like a burglar. The keys, the door handle, the circulars in the mailbox, she muffled everything that could be muffled. When the light from the hall flooded into the kitchen and she caught sight of me she slammed the door shut. Her shoulders shot up and she hissed like a Chinese cobra.

TUSCANY

Winter sun. We were learning the ten-finger method in the school's computer lab. You didn't have to type fast as long as your fingers were correctly positioned.

In another computer lab, Hieu was drifting off exploring the beaches of Tuscany. It didn't take long for him to decide – no more than the time required to compare Tuscany's beaches with the Norwegian coast or Buenos Aires ('despite its position on the Atlantic coast, Argentina's capital offers no swimming whatsoever... the closest beach is several hours away... foreign tourists who arrive in the hottest summer months ask where everyone's gone...') or Dubrovnik. Dubrovnik looked charming, never windy, ideal for romantic excursions, but there was something about Tuscany's beaches, red parasols with aluminium poles, large pebbles in the clear, green water. He decided that at the end of the school year we would go on holiday to Tuscany.

I'll tell Má.
What are you going to tell Má.
I'll tell her that you want it too.

He would ask and she would respond, there was nothing anyone could do about it, but in order to satisfy my curiosity I went to the computer lab myself. At this time anyone could use it during breaktime and after school.

Tuscany...
The promenades...

The cypresses...
The beaches...
The sharp lines between water, sand, and cliff; sudden drops, large bushes. Má would make an impulsive suggestion: we'll take a detour to Pisa and the leaning tower and take a family photo, some friendly stranger will do us the honour, we'll take the bus back, stop at an inlet with shingles and then, the rest of the evening: beach, beach seashells, beach tennis, smoked shrimp on the beach.

The next morning. Má had just washed her face, was barely awake yet, when we told her.

My friend went to Hong Kong... She was never the same again...

Hieu interrupted her. The mild breeze... Cypresses, olive trees... Why was she talking about some friend in Hong Kong?

We can't do that right now, do you understand? We can do something else, we can go to the movies or the pool, but Italy — no.

Hieu and me sharing a room — some nights it was a bigger deal than others. He twisted and turned, violently, talked without words in his sleep. I imagined his dreams: *white clothes, servers — What can I get you, sir? — spaghetti, mussels, rows of set tables, hotels with fans, aquariums, balconies with views, birds, the kites on the beach with the waves and the shrubs, soda; Má's arms under a white, strong sun, the hair turning brown, then yellow like the sand.*

LAURA

We could hear Hieu and Laura all the way from the yard. A loud, expansive laughter. We were defenceless. Má would go stand at the mirror and fix her hair, I would turn on the TV – their light steps in the stairwell, outside the apartment door – and then, 'hello,' cheeks red from the cold. They tossed their backpacks on the floor and pried off their shoes on the hall mat, lifting their faces.

Laura!

Má at the mirror, tense, practically vibrating. An embarrassed, barely audible laughter. A swift glance. Laura had come today, again, yet another day with Laura. Outside the window the winter sun looked like it was sparkling.

Laura and Hieu in the hall, ruddy, a little sweaty in their heavy jumpers.

Laura with the red hair and the dimples.

Laura with the knits.

Laura with the deep voice.

But above all: Laura with Hieu at her side, close by or at her heels, beaming.

Má made cake for the first time. Egg, white chocolate, farmer's cheese, powdered sugar. She melted the chocolate in a tin bowl. She cracked three eggs, separated them into yolks and whites – drew out this moment, all of it took a long time, a rare unhurriedness for Má.

It was one of the first times Laura came home to us. Má met them, she was there and Laura and Hieu were there, in the hall, Má with her hands folded behind her back, not speaking but tilting her head in invitation to the kitchen, she had a surprise waiting for them. Her breathing was heavy. Laura giggled. What a lovely smell.

Laura had dimples. It was something Má pointed out often, she liked to remind us of them, of Laura's dimples.

Laura's dimples, what was it about Laura's dimples? They brought out Má's endless generosity.

She asked Laura about school, about her family, about her hair. Laura asked her about the laundromat, about the flowers in the kitchen, and Má laughed in embarrassment. Did Laura really believe those were real flowers on the windowsill? Those bright colours in this climate – Má knocked with her fingers on the hard, dry soil and shook her head. The flowers looked exactly the way they did the day we bought them.

It was a beautiful cake, round and fluffy and yellow, with a layer of powdered sugar decorating the slightly darker, cooked surface. It was the first time we used the cake forks we had been given by Gunnel.

Gunnel's forks with floral decorations cut through the fluffy cake. Laura praised Má. The cake was still warm. Laura chewed and talked at once: it was incredible, she had never eaten anything like it. Má laughed heartily at this. Hieu looked out the window.

MUKAMAS

Our teacher Anna-Leena gave an impassioned speech about the unique position of the Swedish language in Finland. She had lived in Helsinki and was horrified by the way they spoke down there, she couldn't understand it, why Swedish speakers with an excellent vocabulary felt they needed to reach for Finnish words and expressions.

My *kaveri*!

Why would you say that?

Anna-Leena wrote on the blackboard: *buddy / friend / pal*.

My buddy.

My friend.

My pal.

'This is better, this is better, and' – Anna-Leena pointed at the Swedish words – 'this is better.'

She paced back and forth behind the desk, from one side of the blackboard to the other, back and forth until she was out of breath. She removed a strand of hair from her cheek. She paused to catch her breath. She was about to move on to something else – something to do with what she'd just said. She had said there was one word in Finnish... One word in particular...

She told us about the Finnish word *mukamas*.

Mukamas, she told us, actually does not have an equivalent in Swedish, so if we absolutely felt we had to use Finnish expressions when we spoke Swedish, which seemed to be the case for people down in the capital, then it should be this one. *Mukamas* expresses doubt. If you say that someone *mukamas* is happy to see you, then that means you don't quite believe it. If you say that a film *mukamas* is good, it means someone might have claimed that it is so, though you aren't so sure yourself.

We spent the rest of the period constructing sentences, Swedish sentences containing this *mukamas*, we had five minutes to do it and then everyone was invited to share their sentence.

Ville, in the front, went first. He said that Urho Kaleva Kekkonen had *mukamas* been a good president. Anna-Leena exhaled – as if by a reflex – through her nose; a scoff or suppressed laughter.

She seemed to have appreciated Ville's statement about Kekkonen, but things quickly deteriorated after that. My classmates had composed useless sentences. One after the other: 'our cat is *mukamas* old', 'my sister is *mukamas* going to be a doctor'... Someone had misunderstood the task entirely: 'Titanic is a *mukamas* movie'... After half of the class had said their sentence, long before it would have been my turn, Anna-Leena ended the class and we were let go before time.

COME IN HANDY

Má bought satin sheets. She tore the old ones off the beds and brought them down to the building's garbage shed, unaware of the phone call that would occur that evening, during which Auntie Tei Tei would imply that a set of extra sheets always comes in handy. That way you don't have to do laundry so often. *No, no, no*, Má said in response, the old ones were useless, especially now that they were downstairs in the garbage room.

The new sheets seemed like they could handle anything. I pushed my elbow into the fabric. Even if I could have pushed through the mattress and hit the floor with my arm, breaking the coils on the way, the sheets would probably have remained intact. Hieu was sleeping. I snuck up to the window. The garbage shed was lit from inside, white light streaming through the iron-barred gate and trickling through the slim planks that made up the roof. Hieu in his new sheets. Eyes closed. The comforter had slipped onto the floor, his fists were tightly bundled and pressed between his legs. I was not to wake him.

I'd started to use a trick I'd learned from a TV show to help me fall asleep. The basic idea was that you'd numb yourself using the power of your mind. You got into bed and scanned the length of your body with your mind, part by part, numbing it. First the toes. Let's say the toes on the left foot. You allowed them to relax, ideally so much so that you no longer had any feeling in them – and once that was done you'd move on, either to the toes of the right foot or up the left side of the body, turning your attention to your left calf. This process took so long that I was usually asleep even before I got to the waist. But sometimes when I did this relaxation exercise – that's what they called it on TV – I experienced a number of strange, fascinating phenomena instead of falling asleep. I could hear the wind even though the window was closed. I heard someone speaking a foreign language, or there was the sound of a low, rhythmic beeping, as if from a faraway alarm. And music: singular drumbeats, the chiming of clocks, entire orchestras. I could see, though my eyes were closed. I saw things that did not exist, that were completely unrelated to the experiences I'd had during the day. I saw unfamiliar faces. There was a recurring vision of three faces in constellation, some kind of triangle, hovering, moving up, down, and sideways, ever-shifting – these were Finnish women's faces – their cheeks and foreheads stretched, their mouths and noses dissolved into each other and took on bizarre shapes in glaring colour, as though they were swimming in sunshine. Sometimes these visions were interrupted by a sudden noise – Hieu grinding his teeth in bed, a car jump-starting on the road outside – but it could be something as little as Má rustling with something in the kitchen, or the neighbours' pipes gurgling, that woke me up with a start. I felt the beating of my heart, and everything was back to normal. For a moment I would be wide awake, and at this point I had a choice to make: if I didn't open my eyes and sit up I'd drift off into something new. A new colour, a new light spreading behind my closed eyes.

Hieu didn't move, he just breathed softly. As part of some kind of game I started to imagine him as a different person; I pictured his face like one of those Finnish faces I'd see floating around in their shapeless, three-part constellation, and it was then, absorbed by this strangely captivating game, that I realised that one of those blindingly white faces belonged to Gunnel.

It happened again: I saw the images, the same images of Gunnel in the snow.

I did not want to think about Gunnel.

Gunnel had shown us the berries.

Those first weeks with Gunnel. The streets and the high-rises. Now and then Má would bring it up, how organised and neat she'd found it back then, that the buildings in our neighbourhood were *lined up* like that. Bright images: a clear, pink sky.

On Christmas Day Gunnel invited us over to the small, wood-sided house where she lived with her family outside the city. Lan Pham was travelling and conversation without her was a challenge. We were served glögg and pastries in front of the fireplace. It was one of the warmest days of winter. Later, right before we left, Hieu stood in front of the kitchen window, which faced the backyard. Má walked up to him, something perplexed about her quick, sweeping steps across the kitchen floor. What could he even be looking at out there in the darkness? The forest? Was he listening for something? They stood side by side by the window, but before she was able to ask him she must have realised that he wasn't observing the shovelled yard or the white car in the snow. He wasn't looking at the sky or the forest or the stars; he was watching his own reflection. He opened his eyes wide, he squinted. He flared his nostrils, he watched the movements of his face in the mirror of the window.

CATARATAS DO IGUAÇU

Laura came over several times a week. Má had begun to enjoy these visits; she always offered a bite to eat and did her best to keep the conversation going. Twice, she attempted a joke.

The first time was when Laura had dinner with us, the first time this had happened. She phoned her mum to ask for permission and promised she would cycle home right away after, before it got too dark. Then: something affected over Má's lips. She shut the door to the kitchen and began clattering the crockery. By the time she called us over everything was ready, the table set and dinner served; omelette and rice steaming on the plates, the lettuce green and shiny, the glasses full of water. And everyone had been given their own set of chopsticks. We sat down and Laura stared at the chopsticks next to her plate. And now it was as if Má could no longer control herself. She tried to conceal her grin with her hand and then she made a snorting sound before promptly reaching into the cutlery drawer to give Laura a knife and fork.

Things had been quite complicated there for a moment. Everyone with their chopsticks, even Laura. That was the funny part.

Sometimes after dinner there would be a bit of food left over – more than you'd want to eat, but less than anyone could be bothered to save. It made the meals long and protracted as we lingered, everyone pitching in to finish that last bit. During one of these meals Má's attempted yet another joke.

We were eating sour fish soup, genuinely sour, with tomato and tamarind. At one point Má dipped a large fish head in the fish sauce and passed it to Laura, held it with her chopsticks over Laura's bowl. Laura looked at Má as the fish sauce dripped from the gleaming, white fish eye. Laura and Má, their mouths open, until Má laughed, a little snort, and placed the head in her own bowl.

Fish, and fish sauce. Those days were soaked in a conspicuous smell of fish.

One day Laura dropped a mug onto the floor. I saw it happen from the sofa. It was the mug with a waterfall design on it. CATARATAS DO IGUAÇU engraved beneath the thunderous waterfall. Now that mug was in pieces underneath the kitchen table and Hieu seemed paralysed. Laura's eyes darted around. They stood there, Hieu paralysed, Laura's eyes darting, until Má came to the kitchen. On the floor: the mug with the waterfall. When you held it up to the sun it came to life and looked like it was moving, trickling with silver – the blue turning white and the white grey – down the winding pattern of the mug, toward its base.

Má was beside herself. She berated him.

Choice, forceful words. He was useless.

She berated him in front Laura.

We used to have four mugs. Now we had three.

Normally it didn't take much for Hieu to blush and direct his attention to the floor, but this time he was looking straight ahead, and suddenly Má understood.

Laura squirmed, she was about to say something, maybe apologise, but Má had already transformed: she peacefully went to get the broom and asked them to step aside, *go somewhere, go watch television with the little one, oh my, watch the splinters, for god's sake*. Then he took her hand. Hieu took Laura's hand while it was still trembling and they left the kitchen, Laura on stiff legs.

THE FACE OF ANOTHER

A few days after the incident with Laura I heard Má talking on the phone. She was speaking in code, strange sentences: *woman in the dunes, the face of another, equinox flower*. The following week a package arrived, addressed to her.

There was a box wrapped in brown plastic tape on the kitchen table. Sender: Sister Bao, a friend in Vietnam. The box contained eleven VHS tapes, among them *Woman in the Dunes, Rikyu, The Face of Another, Equinox Flower*. The tapes were old and dented but the labels were new, indicating title, director, and year in neat script, even for *Late Spring*, whose damaged plastic case barely closed.

She watched the films over a short period of time, methodically and without taking breaks.

Later, when she began renting the films to the Vietnamese in town, she'd sometimes be required to say something about them. She'd often focus on some tiny detail, for example when someone asked her about *Late Spring* and she homed in on the scene where Noriko and her father go to the theatre: *the masks, so beautiful, and frightening...*

Sister Bao was an educated person and the films she had sent were strange – slow, often tragic – but as it turned out, this was not a problem. The phone rang incessantly. Má seemed level-headed about the whole thing, even when the film fans bothered her, whether early in the morning or late at night.

Film. Dubbed in Vietnamese. Word got around. The Vietnamese were famished.

They rang the doorbell.

Uyen showed up to rent *Tampopo*.
Ngoc Anh rented *Late Autumn*.
Cuong rented *Ugetsu*.

Thao was bedridden but absolutely wanted to see *Tokyo Story* so Má walked over to deliver by hand. Afterwards, late in the evening, Thao called, snivelling.

For some time every single film was rented out. No more movies to re-watch again, no lines to commit to memory, no soundtracks in the living room. Má was restless.

Hieu and I took it upon us to go to the video store to rent films she wanted to see.

The first time at the video rental; the colours and smells. I quickly learned to enjoy the sharp odour of plastic that hit you the minute you stepped through the door. The VHS tapes were neatly lined up, shelves and shelves of them. It was like a library but with VHS tapes in shiny cases instead of books and newspapers. You were allowed to laugh and talk. Hieu called my name from a hidden corner and held up a movie with an almost naked woman on the cover. We walked around the store for a full hour and there was an intense, salty taste in my mouth that wouldn't go away no matter how many times I swallowed.

With time we learned to ignore the sections for drama, action, comedy, horror, suspense, and documentary, because those never had dubbed movies. The foreign films section and the classics section adjacent to it – that's where we focused our efforts, though it turned out there were only four Japanese films dubbed in Vietnamese in the store. We had no reason to come back. But then Hieu figured that it might not matter where the films had been made, so we tried twice more – first with a contemporary American love story, a blockbuster with Julie Delpy on the cover, and then a French classic from the 60s, both dubbed in Vietnamese – but both times she turned it off at the opening scene.

It took the Vietnamese a few weeks to watch the eleven films. They couldn't resist. Not even *Onibaba*, where a mother-in-law and her daughter-in-law make a living by murdering and robbing samurais in the fields. The women, the silvery grass swaying taller than them; they can't see much farther than a foot in front of them in their stakeout where they wait for the next victim. A sudden movement in the grass.

Several renters balked at the newspaper clipping that had been glued to one of the tapes: PRIMAL EMOTIONS & DARK EROTICISM. They said no thank you, this one was not for them. But a few days later they'd call to ask if they could come pick it up, immediately. They were added to the waitlist.

Film in Vietnamese.

They couldn't resist.

THE BEST DAY

It had snowed. In the morning kids scampered over the sparkling ground, flopping and rolling around. Rosy cheeks. Snow angels, snowballs. It was the first snow of the year. Laughter echoed across the yard. Ticking, frozen tree crowns. It wouldn't be long before the snow ploughs started blinking and scraping in the dark mornings. Sometimes they would drive right by the wall of our building, sending a dull, slowly pulsing yellow light through the blinds. Later all of it would melt, it would happen fast, over the course of a single day, and we'd be stuck with slush penetrating shoes and trousers, settling everywhere with its sour smell. This would be followed by a day of slush turning to ice, roads becoming slippery and uneven. Then again, in mid-October: falling snow, powdery snow, you would tilt your face upward, close your eyes and swallow, drink the black sky.

That winter Timo Maliniemi threw a birthday party. He lived with his mum in a cramped ground-floor apartment, right by the small park behind the video store. The whole class was invited, even Max who had switched schools and a year in still did not have a single friend. The only known fact about Max was that he had rich parents.

Timo grunted at the sight of his wrapped presents. He handled them carefully, inspected them, moved his palms over the patterned papers, caressed their curled ribbons, tapped them with his nails. It was as though he wanted to sit with the rustling for a bit before finally tearing the presents open with a groan.

It was a normal party with chips and candy and birthday cake. Fanta. Salted sticks, which people actually did eat in the end. Max's present was an enormous Lego set: a fire station with an office, a watch tower, and fire trucks in a separate garage. A decidedly advanced set. I gave Timo a case of pens: twelve chunky markers for 25 markkaa. This too made him happy. He grunted and groaned. A wild look: Timo gazed at the ceiling as if it were the sky and proclaimed that this was the best day of his life.

YOU'RE MATCHING

Coffee dates, trying on clothes. Má and Lan Pham took liberties.

What it had come to: Hieu was out with Laura, Má was taking a long shower, Lan Pham's wooden clogs came across the plastic carpet in the living room and subsequently through the foyer right outside our bedroom. She flung the door open without knocking. I was reading with one leg under the covers, the other on top.

Biology. I turned the book and showed her the spread about crows, it was a clumsy movement, my arms crossed at the wrists, fingers sprawled in a strange, unsteady grip. Lan Pham in the doorway, her face half blocked by my book, one of my legs above the covers; the foot, the knee, the thigh, all the way up, the entire leg on top of the covers. *Crows,* she said, and in the same breath, going to the kitchen: *Your mother and I are going to the avenue for a little coffee at the café.*

I sat up on the edge of the bed, focusing on that single spread: the crow, the nearly pitch-black jackdaw, the black and white magpie, the large raven, the rook, the Siberian jay; and the nutcracker, quite rare. A matte, grey light through the quivering blinds.

Má had finished showering. The two of them were having a relaxed, barely audible conversation; a murmur which now and then grew in volume and broke through the din of rummaging and scraping, the snapping of their compacts and lipsticks.

Lan Pham's piercing voice.
You're matching, it's important to match!

she said, and:

What a lovely afternoon for a little coffee at the café!

They walked, shoes on, to the kitchen to fill their water glasses, then swiftly retraced their steps to the bedroom where they were going through Má's closet – *no, not that one* – and when it seemed like they'd finally made up their minds they stepped onto the balcony to check the temperature, just to be sure, and thank God that they did, what a lucky strike, because it turned out they'd dressed far too warmly! High sun and blue skies and the two of them on the balcony pointing at one lightly dressed woman after the other. Their giggles were so ferocious that Má bent over, she bent her knees – a curtseying gesture – and lightly supported herself on Lan Pham's arm. It was a strangely warm winter's day.

Later Má came into the hall wearing tights and a long, red cotton dress.

Lan Pham, enchanted: *Yes, yes, that one!*

They emptied their glasses and left.

I put on my brown lace-up shoes and ran into the lift. I stood between them and we watched each other in the mirror, squinting in the sharp fluorescent light.

Lan Pham's uneven teeth.

Má's red dress and her flickering, red lips.

I inhaled their sweet perfumes.

She had come out of the darkness, Lan Pham. It had started with phone calls, fumbling conversations of few words, the cord snaking along the arm, in and out of Má's hands. She was *just going to call* Lan Pham, in passing. Lan Pham, who had worked as an interpreter. Lan Pham, in youthful makeup, in studs and leather, her heart-shaped sunglasses on her smoke break, at the card table, across from Mr Tèo. Worldly Lan Pham, who had left Vietnam to go all the way to Norway, and finally moved to Ostrobothnia. That time she'd come to assist us. The girlfriend. Now she was back.

FREE HER

It was as if the rekindled friendship with Lan Pham had unlocked something in Má. She moved through the rooms with unusual ease. She talked to Hieu and me about trivial things: the weather, the neighbours, what was on TV.

One day she asked if I might be interested in coming with her to visit Auntie Tei Tei after school. Má was in a good mood that morning. Her hair was newly blow-dried and she nodded to the beat of the music from the TV. She cocked her head and said that Auntie Tei Tei had become *addicted – to film*.

Ghiền phim.

Was this a mission?

Má turned her gaze away from me and returned to her chores, still smiling.

I packed my school bag.

All day I walked around thinking about Auntie Tei Tei.

Ghiền phim...

Auntie Tei Tei and her family came to Finland the same time we did, she'd always been part of our life. But this day would be the first time I truly saw her, in a way that hereinafter allowed me to distinguish her from other Vietnamese adults. She was shy. She rarely spoke. She was several years older than Má. I knew she lived in Kråkholmen, in one of the high-rises by the tracks where a slow, loud train stacked full with timber passed by every day.

Addicted – to film...

We went as soon as school was out.

Auntie Tei Tei's husband opened the door. His quivering

moustache: the mightiest moustache in the family, grizzled and thick like a painter's brush. He offered us soda with ice and lemon, he gave me a big glass. Má said no thanks and instead marched straight to the living room where Auntie Tei Tei sat in the armchair, relaxed, her arms open. One of the Japanese films. It had just started, she said. Má crouched next to the armchair. They looked peaceful somehow, the two of them.

Auntie Tei Tei with her lethargic gaze.

She'd become addicted and we were here to take the movie from her – she was in on it, it was all above board, but before turning it off she wanted to show us a scene.

Here, soon.

She sat up straight, hands resting on her knees. Then her husband scoffed behind us. I turned around and saw him leaning against the door frame, arms crossed. A little smile. He knew the scene. Má and I knew it, too. We had seen the movie several times. *The End of Summer*. Auntie Tei Tei signalled to us to pay attention.

Look, look!

Two men and one woman at a table in a bar. The woman gets up to take a phone call. The men stay seated. One, who is already smoking, is about to light the other's cigarette. They're tense, they're skittish with giddiness. As he lights his friend's cigarette – two hands on the lighter – the flame erupts, incredibly tall, the flame takes over the entire screen, an impressive flame, very tall, powerful – macabre! – but nobody in the room seems to notice. The men take a first drag on their cigarettes. They order three drinks for their table.

Auntie Tei Tei chuckled in her armchair. Má laughed, too.

Following this scene with the men and their cigarettes, Auntie Tei Tei turned the TV off. Her eyes had tears in them. She tried to smile, and Má asked why she was crying. Auntie Tei Tei replied that she wasn't crying. She put the VHS in a plastic bag, and we took the bag home. Her husband had been concerned, he'd asked us to come, Auntie Tei Tei would stay up all night, just sitting there, in front of the movie, he'd said it would be good if we could come and *free her*.

Free her! From a movie!

On the way home I asked Má why Auntie Tei Tei had been crying. She didn't respond, and when we were almost there I asked again.

Why had Auntie Tei Tei been crying?

Má did not answer this time either.

The End of Summer wasn't even a particularly sad movie.

Was it the music?

Was the music sad?

I knew so little about Auntie Tei Tei. I'd been told that she had incredible stamina for work, that they'd called her *a robot* out in the forest, that first summer when they were out picking blueberries.

The End of Summer.

Má and I had freed her from the film.

TAMPOPO

Má and I watched *Tampopo* many times. Assisted by three noodle experts, Tampopo strikes out on his own to open a noodle restaurant. No detail is too small to escape scrutiny. Tampopo throws himself headlong into the project.

> *Look the guest in the eye when you welcome them; look at the guest even when the guest does not look at you.*
> *Is the guest in a hurry?*
> *Is the guest hungry?*
> *Is the guest a new guest?*
> *Is the guest drunk?*
> *Is the guest a guest you want?*

Sometimes we invited Hieu and Laura to our screenings. Má made it sound like an invitation to a festive event – *Tampopo! A timeless feast for the senses!* – and one evening Hieu and Laura did join us. We ate noodles afterwards and it was as though we were staging the film: slurping, burping, handling the pork with extravagant reverence. After that time – the only time – Laura and Hieu almost exclusively sequestered themselves in the bedroom.

Má and I watched *Tampopo* with the sound on high, sometimes so loud that it drowned out everything else. We had a particular appreciation for the scene where a guest, having eaten his noodles, slurps up what remains of the broth; a symbolic act signifying that Tampopo had finally mastered the endlessly complex art of noodle-making.

A timeless feast for the senses. Hieu and Laura had watched it with us one single time.

Long silences from inside the bedroom. Sometimes, when Hieu and Laura were in there, Má behaved strangely. She slammed the doors, rattled the china in the cupboards. One day she put on her heels and walked back and forth in the apartment. She pursed her mouth, she walked back and forth, paused, kept stomping.

We began to walk, Má and I. Furious walks through the snow. She brought the camera.

The final rays of evening light. The trees, and then the clouds. Má in heels.

We walked around the block, down to the water, and the snow fell.

The illuminated, tree-lined streets. The wind in the tree crowns, the white branches. We were already there. Farther down, the lake with its frozen water, indistinguishable from the roadway.

On our way home we paused by a red car parked in front of the fire station. I leaned against the car and smiled in the pool of streetlight. Má shivered. She blew on her hands, first one, then the other, to warm them. The snow whirled and she fumbled with the camera.

Laura had helped me with my homework.

Laura was a good teacher. Clear, concise, knowledgeable.

Laura was interested in Russian poetry.

We had watched television together.

She had asked if I was in love with anyone.

INDEBTED

Months of movie rentals. Hieu had been tasked with chasing down the money owed by Loc. A slowly accumulated debt. Loc had seen all the movies but he hadn't paid for a single one and now he finally had the money.

It was a long afternoon. Hieu was away for several hours and came back without the money. Loc hadn't been home. Má looked confounded. She asked Hieu to repeat what he'd just said.

Nobody was home.

Loc was supposed to be home. Just hours prior Má had talked to him on the phone and he'd told her he would be home all day. Perhaps Hieu had gone to the wrong house, rang somebody else's doorbell. Má decided to go on her own. It was, after all, to her that the debt was owed. She selected her clothes carefully, she took her time, it was getting dark by the time she left, she took the lift down, but before she'd left the building Hieu opened the apartment door and yelled down the stairs so that the entire hallway echoed. He was asking her to come back up.

And now here they were, at opposite ends of the hallway. Má in jacket and shoes. She still looked confounded, curious almost, something lively about her mouth.

And Hieu began to tell his story.

He took a long time explaining it.

Loc had been at home. Hieu had been given the money in a small envelope that he brought to the supermarket.

First he'd been winning.

What?

He was winning at first.

What did he win?

Má waited patiently, up until the mention of the slot machines, when her eyes silenced him. She got the broom. Hieu fell to his knees and stayed like that, for a long time, on his knees, while Má beat him with the handle of the broom. He escaped at first, it was as though he could predict where the strikes would land and she missed, but then: a strange gleam in her eyes, she raised the broom almost all the way to the ceiling, geared up, then hit his bare arms with every strike. He held his breath, tensed up each time, did his best not to make a sound. He was frozen in place, standing on his knees, halfway up on his feet. I stood in the kitchen and watched him crumble. He slithered. He lay with the back of his head pressed against the closet and Má hit him over the legs.

She beat him until he whimpered. Then she went to her bedroom and Hieu lay motionless in the foyer. It wasn't before me he had been kneeling, but he had been kneeling also before me.

A few months. Then Má rewound the movies and put them in a new, brown box. The VHS tapes were to be returned to Sister Bao. One final phone call and the business closed. With time the Vietnamese people stopped coming, but whenever I spotted one of them on the street, or heard someone say an unfamiliar Vietnamese name, I pictured them flocking to our house, standing downstairs once more, yearning. Their cheeks flushed and ablaze.

THE DAYS WITH LAURA

Some Fridays Má had already left for work when I came home from school. A door cracked open, the vanity tidy. Shiny sink, polished mirrors. She had left without a word.

She entrusted me to them. You might sum it up that way: Má entrusted me to Laura and Hieu.

The days with Laura and Hieu. Laura and Hieu at the kitchen table, in each other's arms, waiting for the kettle to boil. Laura's way of looking at the ceiling while she spoke. Hieu repeated parts of her sentences, said yes, said no, said maybe, laughed softly into her ear. Sometimes, when he had his back turned, doing the dishes, filling the teapot with freshly boiled water, Laura would approach him, slowly, almost creeping, and then she'd gently wrap her arms around his waist. Her clavicles against his shoulder blades, her crossed arms in front of his chest. They were standing absolutely still, eyes closed, in some kind of preparation. And then – in a very slow motion, barely moving at all, she lowered her face into his neck as though into a water-filled sink.

Laura!

Impossible to maintain composure.

Laura, behind Hieu, her eyes closed, kissing his neck. Then: resting her head on his shoulder. At this she tilted her face to the side, backwards – to look at me?

The days with Laura and Hieu, when Má left without a word. The yard abuzz with action, families in the midst of their weekend activities. Snow sleds.

I studied. I watched TV with the sound turned down.

Laura and Hieu inside the bedroom: thuds, giggling. The long silences that followed. I was outside, as if waiting for something. Now and then the door opened, and someone came out — Laura or Hieu, never the two of them together — to use the bathroom, to go to the kitchen, to drink some water, grab a fruit, stand for a while at an open window.

Laura: somewhat hurried, barefoot. Once I watched her as she quickly snuck into the bathroom.

IRRESOLUTE

On an early evening in late November, as Laura was lacing up her shoes, Má asked if she was really going to bike home. It was so dark and cold out there. Laura hesitated, and Má asked the same question again, her voice very soft. Finally, Laura went to the phone by the hall mirror, clearly irresolute. Was she going to call? Was she not? Laura's trembling eyelashes. We stood around her, waiting, Má with a toothbrush in hand: a new, pink toothbrush in translucent plastic.

When Laura finally decided to bike home, Má said that she understood, of course she understood, but it would probably be best if she left right away since it was so dark and cold outside.

They waved goodbye through the open kitchen window.

When Laura had unlocked her bike and pedalled away, Má leaned into the cool air and let her arms hang over the windowsill. The woozy light of Laura's dynamo disappeared in the night like a firefly.

Hieu and I shut our bedroom door. It was long before bedtime and we lay in our beds, each facing a wall. When I shut my eyes the image appeared in my mind still, in focus, as though in a dream but without the dream's fickle turn of events: Laura and Má, staring at each other in the bathroom mirror, brushing their teeth – the sluggish, coordinated movements of their arms – until Laura breaks eye contact, suddenly, abruptly, letting her eyes wander across the mirror to meet mine.

Laura was on her way home, all the way to Pörkenäs, on the other side of town.

The sound of doors closing in the yard. Crying children.

Heavy snowfall embedded us in night, but when the stillness was at its deepest, right before the ploughs would come and start scraping outside the window, that's when we woke up. The sound of the sofa being pulled over the floor, stopping with a thud in front of our door.

Má: agitated in the living room.

Hieu sat up in bed, wide awake, bundled in his comforter, red eyes, moist lips. He was sweating.

THIN SHEET

When Laura left Hieu, it was two weeks until Christmas Eve. It happened in conjunction with a strange event involving Laura's sweater, an event that caused Má to lock herself in the bathroom and punch the sink twice in quick succession.

Christmas lights in the high-rise windows. Green and red crosses, anchors, and hearts.
  Hieu was on the move during these dark days. Inexplicably energised. He rummaged through the freezer, found a bag of corn that he cooked in the microwave and then slashed open with a knife. He went to sit on the balcony and ate straight from the package. The autumn term had almost come to a close. On his bed, on the desk, in the apartment: no trace of a single one of his course books.
  It always startled with giggles in the yard. This was how it went when they came, Hieu and Laura, they tended to give advance warning, but on this day Hieu had stayed home and Laura showed up when school was out, in the early afternoon. On this day she had to ring the doorbell.
  Má embraced Laura, who immediately told Má that she would need to leave early, very early, as her bike was at the shop and she would need to take the school bus home. Having informed Má of this, Laura went to see Hieu. Everything was normal, but soon – she'd barely shut the door behind her – she came back into the hall, and that's when Má was standing there, ready, with the sweater.
  Laura basically rotated between three knit sweaters: grey,

yellow, and pale green, one more pilly than the next. Now Má had the pale green sweater in her hands. She was holding it by the shoulders, shaking it lightly, and she informed Laura that a few days prior she had brought it to the laundry, where she'd washed it with the clients' clothes, in the delicates wash, set up specifically for wool garments.

A nice lemon fragrance, she continued, and Laura answered yes, how nice. Then Laura went to Hieu's room again, a quick stop, and just as quickly she came back, descended the stairs, and disappeared around the bend in the road.

Though it all happened in front of my eyes it was somehow impossible to see it clearly: Laura went to back Hieu's room, one last time, and then she left the apartment almost unseen; she slipped by, like a very thin sheet, from the bedroom where Hieu was, through the hall where Má and I were standing. Then: a soundless exit, and she was gone.

Afterwards: the bedroom door wide-open. Hieu's blanket on the floor. He was standing in the centre of the room, his face buried in the pale-green wool cloth.

Eerie snow sculptures in the yard.

Hieu shook his head.

Laura was on her way to the bus stop, and we watched from the window, Hieu and I, until she vanished in between the trees out there.

Crosses, anchors, and hearts in the high-rise windows.

The ploughs.

We sat down, Hieu with his head between his arms; his blue-veined arms stretched over the kitchen table. Má put on the kettle. She sniffled. On her way to the bathroom she hid her eyes in her hands. You could hear how she blew her nose in there, washed her face, and thereafter: a short, metallic clanging, the same sound twice in quick succession.

She returned to the kitchen with her swollen eyes, her face shiny with lotion. Hieu and I were still at the table, dead silent, unmoving. She filled the teapot and put out mugs. Thereafter, leaving the kitchen, she brought three fingers to her lightly pouting lips, and with these three fingers she touched Hieu's forehead. I filled my mug and began to drink the steaming tea. Hieu's empty gaze. The lindens by the motorway. It was the last time Laura came over.

Hieu locked himself in our room during the days that followed. The blankets were halfway to the floor, exposing some of his thin body and his pale, drained face. A movement like a pendulum beneath the eyelids.

Finally Má gave him a talking to.

It was early one morning, a school day, and he let his alarm clock ring. Má marched loudly through the hall and threw the door open.

You have to pull yourself together, she said, and:
Those white girls…
They don't know what it is to love…

During those days of Hieu was curled up in foetal position, dreaming while awake, and I stood over him, watching his tense arm, unmoving and pale on top of the thin blanket. I was sometimes struck by a desire to curl up behind him, to snuggle up along his crooked back.

This desire would calcify. I had to pull myself together, I had to resist it all.

ABSOLUTELY TERRIBLE

On New Year's Eve people gathered on the square, beneath the new year's sky. Má and I stayed home. At one point I heard her crying in the bathroom. A strange kind of sobbing. She didn't open her door all night.

The noise from the yard kept me awake. Hieu's bed was empty again. When I went into the kitchen Má was sitting there with the teapot on the table, and that would be the first time she shared the anecdote about Hieu.

This incident had occurred back when we had a stereo and loudspeaker, as well as – apparently – a karaoke system: a microphone and CDs with Vietnamese songs. Má had tried to make Hieu sing. She said *sing something and I'll give you 20 markkaa*, but he didn't want to. She tried again: *sing something and I'll give you 30 markkaa*, but he didn't want to. Then she pretended to go down to the basement to fetch something. She left the apartment, walked down the steps – *you know, stomping, so he'd hear* – and then she crept back up again and waited at the door. She was beginning to feel silly and was about to go in again, but right then he began to sing. He was singing!

And it was absolutely terrible! Oh, oh! So bad!

I already knew that we used to own a sound system. Má had told me about the time when Gunnel drove us to the industrial area. It was a week after we got here, when the apartment was empty and we didn't even have a sofa to sit on and our bags were yet to be unpacked. Gunnel opened the door to a basement area and all of a sudden we found ourselves in front of a sea of junk: furniture, stuff, clothes. Chairs, beds, lamps, standing fans, pots, china: everything a household might need. Má had given Hieu permission to pick one thing he wanted, and he chose a sound system – two large, black speakers with the amp to go with it, and a couple of records. Gunnel drove it to our apartment along with our new belongings. From that day on we listened to music. Hieu luxuriated in it, Má told me. His pride was palpable whenever a record was on: there would've been no music in our home had it not been for him. He danced: hands in the air, rigorous footwork, hips in constant motion. And I took after him, Má said. I danced, usually sitting in my chair, flapping my arms like two bony wings, twisting my wrists, wriggling my hips back and forth. Sometimes, Má told me, I was even moved by the music when she was putting me to bed. The slightest sound, even a hum or a squeak, could yank me from slumber to wide-awake in one second. And then I'd lie there, staring at her, and she knew I was straining to hear Hieu's slow singing and his precise dance steps in the living room.

Music brought life into our home, but it would end with Má hauling the sound system up to the attic storage space.

There had been one rule: loud music was not allowed in our household, not under any circumstances. Despite this rule she would sometimes notice, upon returning from her language class or the grocery store, that the volume dial had been turned up during her absence. She didn't comment on it, it was all the same to her as long as she didn't have to hear it and as long as the neighbours didn't complain. She was disappointed, however, she told me, not that Hieu had disobeyed her, but that he hadn't been clever enough to turn the dial back after his clandestine listening.

Ultimately she arrived at a decision: the sound system was going to the attic.

Má returned to this anecdote about Hieu's bad singing voice once more, when we were in Kokkola. It was during the big winter sale and we were jostling from one store to another. There was music: rhythmic, rousing music, turned up loud. She launched into the story, and I pre-empted her. I pictured the scene as it must have been: he was sitting on the wooden chair with his legs straight and his feet on the floor. He held the microphone very close, so close that its cold membrane touched his mouth, and he kept his eyes closed as he sang.

LITMANEN

On a rainy day I made an important decision. There was a crowd at the petrol station, with children running around the pumps, laughing and tugging at the hoses. An elderly couple picked up their chairs from the outdoor dining area and carried them in front of their bodies. Right next to the pavement, right where the roof ended and the rain started, that's where they put their chairs. They sat down to watch the storm. The walls of the buildings grew darker. I walked along the empty courtyards. Little bikes had been abandoned on the lawn. The sudden downpour had emptied the neighbourhood of people, but on the street outside our house, right by the curb, I saw a man. He was stooping, and his long, dark hair lay slicked over his leather jacket. Shoulder blades bulging, he looked like he was caught in a tug-o-war: tense neck, hair pulled back, bulging face. Absolutely still, looking at the ground in front of him. A car slowed down, veered to pass him, then accelerated to make the green light. By the man's feet, next to the storm sewer, was a dead rat – halfway dissolved, almost hollow – turned on its back, bare and colourless like a palm. Water whooshed straight through the body and down the drain. I kept walking. I passed the long-haired man. I looked over my shoulder, I saw his face, and I made the decision to quit football.

The man was not staring at the rat. He was resting his eyes on it. Rain poured over his forehead, over his sluggish eyes, and he didn't move a muscle.

The shiny, black hair slick over his shoulders.

He looked like Jari Litmanen.

A week later Olavi phoned me at home. He told me I shouldn't quit, that I 'was going places'. I said I'd already made up my mind. He told me I 'had something'. Receiver pressed to my ear, I was astonished by this obvious untruth. Why was he lying? I pictured them zooming forth: Markus, Erfan, Roman, they were all faster, stronger, more agile than me. They had played in the youth leagues and won competitive games, all of them, their futures were so clear that there was no question of anything else. Olavi was stubborn. Before we said goodbye I promised to think about my decision.

I had already moved on, it was an uncomplicated break, but on the night of Olavi's phone call I did go over a few sequences from the most recent game, the one that would be my last. It was an away game, and we were playing a team from Nedervetil. Strange names were shouted from the bench. Ugly players, ugly jerseys. I crushed them – twice.

I didn't need to do anything at all. It started with a corner kick, the first of the game. I was running for the goal line, requesting a short pass. Juuso lobbed it to me and once I was sure the pass was hard enough, I knew I could do it: keep rushing towards the ball, prepare for the shot, and then, when it was at my feet, do the unexpected, which is to say do nothing at all, just let it roll through my legs. With half of their team tensed for my shot, the ball slipped past them mockingly into the penalty area where Besnik was standing, ready to whisk it in. 1-0.

Then, a breakaway in the second half. It was three against two, Juri with the ball on the right-hand side, me in the middle, chased by both of their ugly centre backs. I got the ball and did it again, I tricked them, I let the ball roll through my legs out to our winger who easily ran through and scored. 2–0.

After the game I got a ride with Jürgen and his parents. I was in the backseat with the shoes and shin guards in a plastic bag in my lap, and we'd barely started moving when Jürgen's mum turned around in the front seat, barely looking at her son. To me: I'd done well, really well.

A mere week had gone by since my decision.

I had stopped playing football. I was destined for something greater.

BEFORE A KISS

A new term. Hieu was rarely home. It's where things were at: he came and went as he wished. I studied at his desk, uninterrupted, with the tree swaying softly in the yard outside.

I had stopped playing football. It wasn't something I would ever regret.

The TV showed images of lonely cities.

Má on the phone, bent over the circulars.

So she had instructed him to get it together.

There was one time when Hieu came home in the middle of the night even though we had school the next day. I woke up from the sound of voices in the hall. It was pitch-black. I extended my foot over the edge of the bed and kicked open the door.

Thin bands of light from a streetlamp fell on Má and Hieu. They were standing just inside the door, Má on the threshold to the kitchen, Hieu at an arm's length from her, still wearing his jacket and a cap. They were facing each other, frozen in place, like dogs, or as though before a kiss.

The silence of the night.

Her hand shot up to his face, a quiver. She disappeared into the kitchen.

He snuck into the darkness of our room.

He paused at the foot of my bed and I immediately smelled the alcohol on his breath. He stood there over me and my feigned sleep. Long, even breaths.

He slunk over to the desk, turned on the desk lamp, and directed the light at his bed. He undressed in the centre of the room: the crinkly jacket, the trousers. I rolled over to face his way, eyes half-closed.

His folded jeans hung neatly over the desk chair. His sharp shoulder blades. Pale, spotted legs. The arm that turned off the light.

He was breathing quickly, in through the nose, out through the mouth.

HERRMAN'S

An uneventful spring. Then, summer. Flies flew in and out through the wide-open windows. Hieu had got a job at Herrman's plastics factory, which manufactured bike lamps. One night he emptied his black leather wallet onto the middle of the kitchen table. It was dusk, right before Má came home from the laundromat, and the two of them spent the rest of the evening counting the money, the same set of notes and coins, again and again. In the days that followed they paced the apartment, Hieu and Má. Whenever they happened to sit down to rest, on a chair or the floor, whenever they went to bed or lay down for a nap, it was as if they were woken by the other looking at them, as if their excitement was always intact and could be found in the eyes of the other. Getting up from their chair or the floor they entered a kind of momentary, augmented wakefulness. Something in their gazes: an immeasurable sharpness, as if a storm had suddenly blown through and covered the room in dew.

It was a boring summer, colourful and endless. Ants and mosquitoes in the empty schoolyard. The grass growing freely. Now and then I bumped into my old teammates and sometimes we played football till late at night. Afterwards I took long showers, alternating between hot and cold, sitting down, standing up in the streaming water.

I had left my team and would never regret it.

I had watched Dennis Bergkamp turn Argentina's poor centre-back inside out with two touches. Then he'd brought the goalie to his knees: vanquished, outsmarted. After his astonishing goal, Dennis Bergkamp had made a run for the corner flag, he'd flung himself on the ground with his arms stretched to the sky, everything was vibrating, I remembered it clearly, the commentators were overwhelmed, all they could do was repeat his name. Bergkamp! Bergkamp!

Bergkamp existed.

I pictured Bergkamp – it was possible, Bergkamp existed – but I had left my team.

These were the nights that never darkened. Summer was in full bloom right there and then, but the images in my mind were all of events from our first summer. The summer of berry picking, when Má and Hieu and Auntie Tei Tei and Lan Pham went to the forest without me. I pictured the sun's burning rays into our apartment, how we went to bed hoping for night-time rain. Gunnel showed them the berries. Then they forgot all about her.

WHAT DO YOU SAY?

The first summer with Gunnel. She calls and exclaims: 'Have you seen! Have you seen all the colours!'

The first summer's unfamiliar weather. Má is used to heat, but the sort of heat that comes wrapped in humidity. This summer is dry and the air is heavy, empty. She wades in restlessness. She opens the curtains, she lets the light in, she pulls them again. She moves the TV, the sofa, the coffee table. Suddenly Hieu and I are at home all day every day and Hieu is moping and complaining about how boring everything is. One day Má decides to do something about it, but she's in two minds, she doesn't know what she wants. She asks if he wants to come berry picking, because if he really wants to do that we can all go together: Má and him and I, Gunnel and Lan Pham. To her surprise he says yes immediately.

Má's indecision has nothing to do with the berry picking itself. The thing is that there's always something extra with Gunnel. She's been thinking about what Gunnel said before, that the air is so fresh out there, and there were also those words that Lan Pham couldn't translate: 'jam', 'cordial'. Má can't remember which is which, just that one is a drink and the other some kind of foodstuff, that both are a mixture of berries and, as Lan Pham put it, *enormous amounts* of sugar.

Má's indecision also has to do with me. We have done everything together, Hieu and I, but an event like this, an expedition, demands *full control*. In other words: you can't have a toddler running around out there.

She can't have me running around out there, but it's too late to cancel. She looks at Hieu, who is bouncing in front of the living room window, his large eyes and large mouth. The plan has already been made, she's promised, and promises come with obligations.

It might be a very long day. Dragging her feet, she calls Lan Pham, and then Gunnel. Lan Pham says yes, sure, she doesn't have anything else on anyway. Gunnel picks up the phone and Má starts by saying something about the weather, it's such a nice day, she's been thinking about that berry picking idea, it sounded so nice, and now she's wondering if a day like today might be suitable or if they better wait and do it later. Gunnel responds that the weather is well-suited for berry picking, in fact it's the best weather imaginable for it. Má brightens. They figure out the transportation.

She makes another phone call: she arranges for me to spend the afternoon at Lan Pham's friend's. I'm going to watch TV in their living room. TV, living room; it's the same thing, barely different from home.

Má is enormously relieved when Gunnel turns up in the car park outside the kitchen window. She is no longer in two minds. Anything but the hot, dry apartment and its bare walls. It is, in fact, a very nice summer day. Hieu has already laced up his shoes.

Five minutes later we are once again in the backseat of Gunnel's car. She drives out of the city centre. She stops at the end of Rådhusgatan, in the car park next to a tall high rise – probably one of the tallest buildings in the city – and Má walks me to the entrance where Lan Pham's friend is ready to pick me up. A kiss on the cheek. Má returns to the others in the car and they drive off.

***

They leave town. Gunnel can't stop talking about how happy she is that they're doing this. She loves picking berries.

They spend the whole afternoon together. Gunnel knows a spot, she goes there every year. This spot has never let her down. She and Lan Pham talk at great length and with much excitement about the Right of Public Access, a principle that says every forest is for everyone to enjoy, and which Lan Pham knows from her time in Norway.

It's blueberry season. Everyone has their own container for picking. Hieu disappears into the forest. He returns with bright-blue lips. He rubs his hands like someone who's just sealed a great deal. Delicious, but now he wants to go home. The mosquitoes, he says, which Má thinks is a perfect excuse. So does Gunnel, because they drive home right away, and to Má's surprise there is nothing extra, no cordials or jams; just straight to Rådhusgatan to pick me up, then each and every one back to theirs.

Later that night, once we're in bed, Má is still restless. She can't be still. She's tossing and turning. Now there is something else, too. She's agitated. She wakes Hieu and whispers by his head: *I think we can do it, we need to call her, tomorrow.*

The next day, as soon as she's up, she phones Gunnel. She asks if Auntie Tei Tei can come too. A few hours later they're in Stefan's, Gunnel's husband's car. They pick up Auntie Tei Tei on the way. They drop me off at Rådhusgatan again. They continue without me.

Gunnel drives down small, scrubby gravel roads. They speak in Vietnamese. Gunnel asks what they're talking about, but nobody replies. After a long silence Má speaks: *I think we're scaring her.* Hieu sniggers. 'What are you talking about?' Gunnel asks and nobody says a word, not even Lan Pham.

She never doubted, but the second she lets the first berries roll in, Má is convinced. Gunnel has supplied them each with a berry-picker – she has several of them at home, all with wooden handles and fine steel netting – and the unquestionable efficacy of these implements silences Má and Auntie Tei Tei. They have not come here to chat. They have been struck by a remarkable enthusiasm, an unspoken mania, manifest in their bent backs. Gunnel and Lan Pham are still standing by the big car, astounded. They watch Hieu disappear in between the trees. When he returns his whole face is blue, his neck and ears.

Later that day Má and Hieu are in the kitchen with two buckets filled to the brim. Má lifts one of them, then puts it down, up, then down, her arm muscles bulge. Hieu does the same with the other. They decide to get scales.

I'LL HAVE EVERYTHING

I didn't spend as much thinking about that first summer once the fall term started. And with the fall term came the days with Lan Pham.

The days with Lan Pham.

The rainy days, the sunny days, the lazy, idle, the quiet days.

The days of laughter, when Lan Pham's voice was the only voice; one single, long day spent together at the coffee house.

Lan Pham had a boyish, nonchalant voice, a voice with the power to make you all shy and embarrassed. When Má and I were at home and Hieu was sneaking around either on his way in or out, it was as if Lan Pham's voice lingered; that delicate pitch constantly commenting on the surroundings, now this, now that, an enjoyable drone that billowed through the room.

Lan Pham had a delicate voice; delicate but not shrill.

Days at the coffee house. Late-summer sun: a stubborn, heatless gleam, too bright to look at longer than in glimpses. Walks down the avenue, past the stores and the restaurants with their rancid smells, soon to be encapsulated and stifled by the winter cold.

But before that: The days with Lan Pham.

Her whims. Sometimes, at the most surprising moments, she had an impulse to scold someone. This happened during our first visit to the coffee house. We'd just sat down in the adjoining pavilion, each with a cup in hand, we'd barely found our seats when the wind picked up and people covered their drinks to shield them from falling leaves. Má complained: *I can't tell, I can't tell if I'm inside or outside!*

It was a nice café with wooden panels and armchairs and a chequered floor; even the light was pleasant: the overhead lights were off and there were floor lamps with thick, patterned shades. We'd chosen a table in the back with a fabulous view of the entrance. Most visitors were properly dressed: blazers, shoes with heels; even an older woman in a hat. Now and then though, someone like the girl with a stroller would come in. She was a little breathless and her hair was tousled and damp from what must have been sweat. She was wearing slouchy cotton trousers and a hoodie.

A hoodie... At a coffee house...

Má and Lan Pham exchanged a glance.

Most patrons made a brief visit – they barely bothered to take their coats off as they absent-mindedly flipped through some magazine, drank their coffee, and left – but next to our table there was a man who appeared to be in no rush. There were two plates in front of him: one with used cutlery and a desiccated half of a lemon, the other with a half-eaten cream pastry. He was talking to one of the waitresses, chit-chatting about the weather. He asked if she liked sports, and if so what kinds of sports. She responded politely and he kept asking. No issues there, everything was in order. He asked and she responded, it was cosy, necessary even – without a bit of background noise it would have been difficult to carry on a conversation – but the thing was that this particular man was absolutely and completely unable to adapt his delivery to the surroundings. There was music in the background, barely audible, people speaking softly, each table to itself, each couple to itself, but this man was something altogether different. We were at the table next to his and it quickly became unbearable.

Whenever he laughed – a laughter that came out of nowhere – it was as if you had to close your eyes and collect yourself. Our attention was inevitably drawn to him. Finally we started commenting on his behaviour.

It was Lan Pham who started it. She spoke loud and clear. Said: that man must not have been breastfed as a baby, maybe that's why he's yelling like that. Má opened her eyes wide. It was her turn. Lan Pham squinted, focused, at the table. Má accepted the challenge. It was her turn and she called him an *unwashed gnome*.

Lan Pham sometimes had a surprising way of carrying herself. It might look strange in the moment, but in the end it always made sense, against all odds, as if she was above the natural order of things and not the other way around.

After Má called the loud man an unwashed gnome Lan Pham got up – a sudden, violent movement, the porcelain rattled – and walked out the door with both hands covering her mouth. Then she stood outside, motionless, turned toward the street. We watched her through the window. The thin cloth of her shirt wafted in the breeze. Everything was dead silent for a moment. No deafening laughter, no din, nobody entered, nobody left.

Was she getting ready?

For what?

I bit my straw. Even the bubbles in my drink were silent.

She came back in with a smile on her face, poured a glass of water at the self-service cart, and walked, her steps loud, towards us. She took a sip, put the glass on the table, and swivelled around so she was facing the man. He looked down at his plates, stirred his coffee, looked away, but Lan Pham did not look away, and finally they saw each other.

'Hey, listen,' she said, and this was a foreign Swedish, soft where it should have been hard, hard where it should have been soft; 'would you like to know what my girlfriend here said about you?'

He raised his eyebrows. Lan Pham sipped her water and continued.

'She said that you're a real clown, that you should stop and think for a second before you talk like that to people who aren't interested. Don't you understand how it sounds, didn't your mother raise you right, the one who didn't breastfeed you?'

She said it all in one go, didn't stumble even once.

Lan Pham sat back down again. We didn't make a big deal out of it, we talked about the weather, about the coffee house's offerings, Lan Pham asked if we'd like to try one of those kinuski pastries. The man finished his coffee. He looked around, confused, thoroughly red-faced, before he got up and left.

Má covered her mouth. What exactly had Lan Pham said?

I blew into my carbonated water and observed the incredible, bubbling foam that resulted.

The eyes of the others.

The faint steps of the man rounding the corner.

Lan Pham walked to the counter to order again.

Lan Pham: I'll have everything.

The confectioner: Pardon?

Lan Pham: Just kidding… I'll have one of those kinuski pastries…

PHOTO PROCESSING

When Foto Elite opened in the City House they were the first business in the building. It was mainly family photos back then. Foto Elite were the first in Finland with a film processor; this was in the sixties. In that era you had to be knowledgeable about chemistry because it involved mixing liquids, and things could end badly if you didn't know what you were doing. Nowadays nobody needed to know anything about chemistry to process film – that process was automated – but technical skills were still a requirement, because the new processing machines were sometimes quite complex. 1978 was a banner year for Foto Elite: the year they started developing colour photos. Up until then, black and white was the thing, so this was a big change.

The storekeeper told Má this history.

It's special, to get to work with people. Best of all, the storekeeper explained, was photographing wedding couples.

'They are so happy... Their eyes have a sparkle.'

Foto Elite used a semi-matte, thick paper stock that gave the photos a nice lustre. They specialised in photo books – and if we were interested the storekeeper had an exclusive offer, just for us.

A very good price...

The storekeeper looked my way; I was regarding the new cameras in the glass case. Má said she just wanted her photos. The storekeeper walked into the backroom and immediately came back with the photos in an envelope. She said it was in fact possible to develop your photos at home if you wanted, in something called a home lab. All you needed was a room that could be made completely dark, like a windowless bathroom. The equipment – chemicals, photo paper, and so on – could be bought at a low cost in their store. The storekeeper passed Má a little book in addition to the envelope, and in that moment, when she handed Má the booklet, she glanced my way again, as if she was passing the photos and the booklet to me, too. When we left the store – it was next to the church and the cemetery, where you'd often see a few people ambling around, reading the headstones – Má gave me the booklet. It was no more than a few stapled sheets of paper; a slim pamphlet with sparse text and pictures of various kinds of machines and photo paper.

PHOTO PROCESSING
This is how processing happens
In complete darkness
In daylight

Nowadays the only time I saw Laura was on a forgotten photo that someone had left in the bathroom cabinet, slipped between the lipstick and toner. She's on the sofa, curled up underneath the white blanket with her eyes closed and her head resting on her interlaced fingers. Her eyes are twitching, she's about to wake up, she's pushing her hair behind her ears.

SISTER FACTORY

Hieu stayed on working at Herrman's after the summer break. Lan Pham came to visit and made coffee using a cone and filter she'd brought from home. Sugar and clattering porcelain. One day she gifted Má a knit sweater from Prada. It was used but in good shape, a stylish latte shade, cable-knit, made in their Russian sister factory. A spontaneous gift, *just because*. The sweater, it turned out, was a perfect fit. Throughout the fall and winter, all the way until spring, Má would wear it at least once a week. *Sister factory. Exquisite collar.* Words spoken by Lan Pham. Má was thrilled.

With Lan Pham, the lively days were the simple ones; days spent about town; easy, unstructured days.

But then came the days when nothing happened. No people, no scents; dull days when we remained quiet. It was as though, then, that Lan Pham wanted something from us. She talked, asked questions, and once she got going, there was no stopping her.

She prattled on.

Romance, infatuation, love letters, unforgettable encounters.

Things that had recently been enjoyable – that same laughter, that same voice, the one that had chastised the man at the coffee house – these aspects now pitched us into a heavy silence. I could see it on Má: her body hunched, her arms crossed over her chest, the void in her eyes as Lan Pham went on about love, always this chatter about love: love films, love songs, the nature of love, the phases of infatuation, surges of the heart.

These were soundless evenings when Hieu was like a ghost appearing only in glimpses; a door opening and softly closing. Once, as we were settling down to eat, I approached him, he was already in his chair, wearing an open shirt. I came closer, regarded the soft curve of his collarbones. I wanted to stroke the shiny fabric of the shirt that wrapped around his shoulders.

One day when I was home alone, a photograph fell out of one of Hieu's books as I was frenetically turning the pages. I was entranced both by the motif and the size of the photo – it covered almost the entire page of Hieu's textbook. Auntie Tei Tei, Má, and Hieu among the trees. The forest, the look of the trees; it was a foreign, almost exotic place. Later when I lay down to sleep that photo came back to me, like a soft yellowish raster in my mind's eye. And again the next day: Má and Auntie Tei Tei and Hieu out there in the forest, Auntie Tei Tei and Má standing, Hieu crouching. The billowing, translucent pine forest. I couldn't shield myself, the image lingered, pursued me like some kind of forbidden secret.

A LOOK LIKE NO OTHER

The photo in question: Auntie Tei Tei, Má, and Hieu in the forest. It's early morning and the image shows neither sun nor clouds. The yellowish haze casts long shadows between the sparse trees; spruces, here and there a pine. They're facing the camera, Auntie Tei Tei and Má each with an arm around the other, Hieu crouching in front of them in his red rubber boots. Oddly enough everyone is wearing red rubber boots and the shoes look polished, like fluorescent lights against the matte backdrop. Má and Hieu are facing the camera head-on, cautious smiles. Blurry branches in the foreground. Long, sharp shadows from the trees. White and yellow spots appear in some places. The viewer must proceed as if hunting, using his eyes to slowly search the picture. What are those – small birds? Insects? Flower petals? Auntie Tei Tei is seeing something far outside the frame. She radiates boundless expectation, it's a look like no other.

They look small, almost shrunken beneath the majestic trees, as if swallowed up by the jade-coloured landscape. A strange formation, like they're a sports team. I had to use all my focus. Hieu's padded grey jacket shimmers in the morning light, as if sculpted in silver. I imagined it out there in the forest. Blueberry brambles, trees, shadows. Auntie Tei Tei looks like a person in love: her attention is fully absorbed by whatever it is she's looking at so longingly, and you might notice a sort of invisible movement around her closed mouth. The upper lip is taking on the contours of a bow being tensed and released, tensed and released.

SUNBIRDS AND COLIBRIS

The seed of everything was planted during those eventful days. Leisurely walks to the beach. Gunnel's silence.

Yes: Gunnel is increasingly quiet. Beautiful, uneventful days. A walk can fill an entire afternoon. We go to the beach a lot. We watch the families who replace one another in the sun. It's early summer: the faint beating of the sea, skin glittering in the waves.

Silence settles; it's not completely silent, but things are very still. The first real berry-picking excursion is still many weeks out, the nights and days they are going to spend in the forest without me.

Hieu and I are sleepless during the hot, dry nights in the city. We've been instructed to never open the window, to never sleep in a draft, but there is one of these hot, dry nights when the air is particularly hard to breathe. Hieu leaves his sleep and opens the window onto the grove. The mosquitoes are ruthless. Má is distraught to see the red marks that cover our bodies the next morning. We scratch and scrape our skin with long strokes, like we're painting, and Má barks. We stay in the same room, close to each other for the rest of the day, on the sofa or by the kitchen table. It's a rare thing. Má keeps watch, stopping us from touching our arms, meticulously scolding us, and when we wake up the following day the bites still itch but less so, and the redness has faded. That night

I dream about sunbirds and colibris with vicious eyes who flutter in and out of the fruit garden, which is in Má's bedroom. It's a beautiful dream, breezy and colourful.

She's on the phone a lot. She sits in a chair by the kitchen window with her legs pulled up under her, looking at the street. She's present, attentive to the goings-on underneath the smooth, dusky sky. She lies about the following things to the girlfriend on the phone: Hieu's schooling, her own schooling, future prospects. She describes the sense of exaltation that's come to her in the new country, how it keeps shapeshifting. This is a lie she's made a home in, and now the false images blend with her hopes. The order is disturbed, even a lie has an internal logic: she shuts her eyes, then opens them, it is seamless.

Hieu and Má stay up one night planning and making calculations, whispering about the future, I can hear it now, not the words but the tone of their voices, I hear the giggles most clearly, it breaks through intermittently, I can't trace it but it makes my heart pound. Hieu turning the pages of the atlas. Má tapping on the calculator. Their giggles. I listen, sleepless in bed. This is how it all begins.

One day, another day, they will drop me off with Lan Pham's girlfriend. They are going back to the forest, Má, Hieu, Lan Pham, and Auntie Tei Tei, they're planning to spend an entire week out there.

FEED

Má came home with a large piece of meat. She sliced it in thin strips. She rinsed the bloodied water from the cutting board and chopped the tomato. Everything was going into the frying pan. A sizzling sound; Má opened the window.

Music drifted in from outside. Hieu reached for the plates while I got cutlery and poured water into our glasses. Intermittently one of us would leave the kitchen to go to the bathroom, change clothes, change the channel, turn down the volume, but most of the time, for long spells, we were in the kitchen together: Má, Hieu, and me, squeezed together, cooking.

Hieu had bought a leather jacket from an older schoolmate. As Má tried the meat one last time he went to the hall to put it on, pulling the zipper all the way up to the collar. The jacket was almost brand-new, black and shiny.

A bed of lettuce wreathed the serving plate. It was topped by beef, onion, and tomatoes, which, combined with herbs, created a mixture that we dipped in fish sauce and then mixed with the rice in our bowls. *This is how it should be eaten.* The lettuce. Má liked it this way: crisp, lightly marinated. We were very hungry. Hieu reached eagerly across the table. Rattling zippers ran down both sleeves of his jacket, starting at the elbows.

Yellow leaves were visible through the window, which remained cracked open.

Music from the yard. Footsteps in the stairwell. Má went to open the door for Lan Pham. They entered the kitchen next to each other, Lan Pham's gaze darting around. She was carrying a wine bottle and three glasses. She'd let her hair grow out to her shoulders.

Má got her a chair from the bedroom. It was the first time all of us were eating together: Má, Hieu, Lan Pham, and I.

Lan Pham got her own bowl and chopsticks. She ate while we watched in silence. After she'd finished a first serving she got up, took the wine bottle from the fridge, and placed it on the table next to the three wine glasses. Apparently it was time for conversation.

She complimented Hieu's leather jacket.

She asked if he was going to get his driver's license soon.

Hieu was silent. He was eating with what might be described as disciplined focus, and when he, after finishing what was in his bowl, reached over the table to grab a large piece of lettuce that he slowly lowered into the fish sauce, Má answered for him: He was just fifteen, of course he didn't have his license yet. Lan Pham unscrewed the cork from the bottle and poured herself a glass of the golden, bubbling wine. She held on to the bottle and glanced at Má, who shook her head. The headshake was small, barely noticeable, but she kept shaking until Lan Pham had returned the bottle to the table.

It was a French wine, with the year written under the French flag. When Lan Pham had drank her first glass and was about to pour another Má tapped her own glass with the nail of her index finger. A third of the way up: that's how much she wanted Lan Pham to pour.

Smattering motorbikes in the distance.

So Má was going to drink wine.

By the time dinner was finished and Hieu was rinsing his plate, Lan Pham returned to the subject of his leather jacket.

She noted that it was real leather, you could tell from the smell. Hearing this Hieu turned off the faucet and spun around to face the table with his back to the sink.

Yes, it really was a luxurious jacket.

Má gestured at him to come closer. She was sitting back in her chair, one leg pulled up so that her foot was resting on the seat. As soon as Hieu was within reach she straightened up and grabbed his arm. She brought her face to his sleeve and smelled it – sniffed it, really, her nose twitching, before letting go. *Real leather*, she said, *it could be Italian*. Lan Pham asked how much he gave for it. Hieu cleared his throat, inhaled, and explained that he got it for cheap since his friend, an older schoolmate, had bought it but changed his mind immediately, just a week later.

Má, with shiny eyes:

What a good purchase.

Hieu fumbled with the zipper to the breast pocket, opening and closing it as if making sure it worked.

Lan Pham adjusted her posture, leaned forward with her chin on her fist.

Why haven't you conditioned the leather?

She was on one. She asked if Má hadn't taught him, underscored that it's crucial to *feed the leather* to prevent it from cracking, otherwise it gets wet in the rain and then it dries and then...

I'll take care of it, you boys go, I'm sure you have homework.

Má interrupted her, and in the silence that followed I got up and we went to our room, Hieu and I.

Má had interrupted her. Lan Pham had been cut off, but after Hieu and I had got to our bedroom we heard her shout

117

something from the kitchen. She was asking about Laura. Hieu shrugged. We had closed the door, it was just him and me in the room and he shrugged.

Lan Pham...

She had called Laura *the redhead*.

Hieu shook his head. He was sitting at the desk with his jacket on. The leather creaked when he shifted.

It got late. After a while the only sounds we heard from the kitchen was murmuring interspersed by laughter. Just before I fell asleep I got up from my bed and snuck out to use the bathroom. There, through the wall, I heard Lan Pham talking, her voice muted but clear.

LAN PHAM'S TIRADE

There are some good spaces down by the port that nobody wants... If you go past the housing expo... Europa, Equator, whatever those neighbourhoods are called... Make it fashionable and people will come, there's parking and streetlights leading the way... You don't believe me! But listen... I promise, in Oslo I knew lots of people my age... Or I guess your age and my age, families... Who owned restaurants... Not that they were serving bánh xèo and bún bò... I'm talking sushi restaurants... The whiteys come and they're spending like it's Monopoly money... You know what they're like, it's all 'nice, nice', they don't care whether you're Japanese or Vietnamese or Thai or Korean... We're all Chinese to them... Hahahahaha... You have to believe me... It was your idea from the start... Honestly you have no one but yourself to blame, you can't propose something and then just... I'm thinking there are a few tricks we could use, like obviously it has to be a good space, cosy and all that, but in order to charge a lot we have to make it upscale... Not like a regular Vietnamese hotel... It should be kind of old-fashioned... Picture this: kind of dim everywhere, scented candles and stuff, but not so scented that you notice it immediately! More like, imagine a scent of green tea, not jasmine, straight up green tea... Slightly bitter... And dark-green panels and wood floors they can walk on in slippers... Green is probably a good colour, generally speaking... Not bright green, obviously... Like 'Kungens gröna kulor'... Hahahaha... That's a Finnish candy made from green marmalade...

I've often received it as a gift, you know, for Christmas, it's absolutely disgusting... Just sugar, nothing else... These whiteys... They're funny... But yeah, dark green... And slippers, we can buy them for cheap and make them available to the guests... Can't go wrong... You already managed a movie rental, you know about the money part, and now you're working at the laundry, it's perfect! Listen, what if we started some kind of hotel business... Excuse me? Calm down? I am calm... What do you mean calm down... You really think we'd be sitting here right now if either of us had calmed down? I think you're being too humble... You know the money part, you know laundry, your eldest can work in the reception after school... Might as well put him to work... You said you'd discussed this with him? Is that right? And he had some ideas of his own... I can imagine... His ideas... They can't be good... But if he could assist with the practical stuff... He's not seeing her anymore? Oh... I knew it, I had a sense... That's too bad, I almost said, too bad I didn't get to meet her... But it's probably for the best... I heard what you told me about her... No, no... Nothing bad, not like that, but there was something, I can't remember how you put it, maybe you said she was bloodless? Or pale? Sure, sure... Bloodless, pale... He'll meet someone else soon... Actually, I ran into him the other day... He was outside Prisma, in the car park, they were sipping on energy drinks, he and his friend... Some Albanian guy... Pretty handsome, I have to say... In any case we chatted for a bit... I tried to teach them how to be with girls... I explained that they need to be direct... Make an impression... Don't be scared! That's it! Don't be scared! Just do it! But that son of yours... He really didn't get it...

Honestly, he looked scared... The Albanian just laughed so I left... I'm sure he'll find someone... Your son, I mean... I'm not worried at all... It's so easy for them... Walk down the street one night and all of a sudden they've found love... Just imagine if it was like that for us... Not even when we were young... When I was young... Yeah, it's going to be fine... You'll have to make sure to condition that jacket... He's so pleased... With that jacket... I know how much these things can mean at that age... I remember when I got my first long dress...I wore it all the time...I slept in it, I barely took it off to shower... After a year the seams came undone... And I had to wait for a new one...Hold on, I just thought of something... Before I forget... You know, maybe we should have kimonos made... Listen! Don't worry, everyone does it, we'll order from China and they'll get here in just a few weeks...Whiteys love that stuff, they take every chance they get...They think they're in America when they're at McDonald's, they pay for expensive spaghetti at Finnish restaurants... And obviously they cheat us all the time...You don't want to know how many underpaid jobs I've had... Kimonos, though... That style with a belt around the waist and a bit of a neckline... Both men and women can wear them, and we'll have to get a few in small sizes too... Just imagine how cute it'll be... Little white children in kimonos, and all of them have paid cover... Have you ever heard of anything so beautiful... Come on... Don't be so anxious... Why do you always look so anxious... And the last thing I'll say... Listen now, because this is pure genius... Outside, at the entrance, we'll have an accent wall, do you know what I'm talking about, an accent wall? That will be the cherry on top or whatever the expression is... This accent wall... It'll be the first thing they see when they get there... Like a greeting... 'Welcome! Nice, nice!' Hahahahaha... And when they leave they'll want to pose and take pictures in front of it... I'm telling you, I know exactly what it should look like, there's Japanese landscape wallpaper, it looks like you're in the countryside, water moving in the river, maybe a temple... Hahahahaha... 'Cute, cute!' They love this stuff... And we'll need to be clever when we serve them, or, what's that word – wise! We'll be wise women from the jungle... I mean the countryside... Hahahaha! You know what I'm saying? That kind of wise woman who says things they've never thought of before, things that sound obvious... Like you shouldn't brew tea in water that's too hot since it makes it bitter... Did you know that? It might just be for green tea... I did hear someone say that though... And we must be self-confident, that's the main thing... And then something along the lines of... This is something I read in a magazine... That when you wash your face with soap... Or, what is it, with face wash... When you're using face wash... Apparently you're supposed to... Like, normally you'd take some of this solution or whatever you call it, this face wash, and then you lather it in your hands, like so, right? But this magazine said that this is not the right way to do it, you're supposed to lather it on your face! You get it? The idea is that something happens in the lathering itself, and if you do it in your hands the hands will receive what the face wants... I don't know if this is true, it sounds so strange... But I've actually started doing it that way... Like... I lather it on my face... I started in the spring, and I still look like this... Could be worse, but... Not exactly a princess... If we open a spa this is something we'll have to consider, you know, we'll have to mind our looks... Drink a lot of water... Start running maybe... Hahahaha... We're going to start running, you and I... Anything for business!

SHE WAS DOING WHAT WE WERE DOING

Every autumn the huge patch of gravel across Skolparken was transformed into a fairground. We walked all the way there, Má and I. Cars and mopeds everywhere, young people's impatient body language. Having arrived, we bought kringla and liquorice strips and ate our treats outside the freshly cleaned windows of the clothing shop. People were flocking to the illuminated tents. Food stands and attractions. Foreigners, young men, parading enormous clutches of oddly shaped balloons.

A woman was standing right near us, by the same store window, alone. One hand resting on a stroller, the other holding a stick of cotton candy. She was doing what we were doing: eating, watching the bustling fairgrounds from the outside.

Má took her picture.

FLUTTERING HEARTS

The photograph shows the woman as one with her stroller. She's bending down so that half her face is inside the stroller's hood. The store window reflects part of the enormous Ferris wheel — its lights, which look the floodlights of a football stadium, cut through the darkness. The woman and the stroller: her head is like a huge rock in a cave opening. From within the protective hood, the baby's bubbling laughter.

Teens roved the fairgrounds in groups. The biggest crowd was clustered around a stand where you shot at various objects with a fake gun. The better the shot, the bigger the prize. The top award was a massive teddy bear. Activities like this tended to draw big crowds: families, kids, love birds.

One of them was a boy with a determined look on his face. He bungled his first two shots, real misses, didn't hit a single can, but on his last attempt he knocked down two out of six. The person manning the stand gave him his prize: a little panda, fist-sized. The boy immediately passed it to the girl who was next to him, and she, in response, leaned in and kissed his neck with her eyes closed. Someone cheered. The boy and the girl traipsed off into the dim fairgrounds. Everything was dark outside the fair, and the carousel lights trembled in the smoke.

The fluttering hearts of young people. They came in hordes, locked their bikes, left them leaning against the fairground fence. They approached the crowds with their strutting, confident gait and it struck me that those boys looked like him: Hieu could have been one of them. I thought about Laura. Did he miss her? I missed her.

FIAT

The days in the backseat of Lan Pham's Fiat, next to the flood-lit trails, on muddy roads that never seemed like they had time to recover from rain. On early evenings we would turn off and leave the river of cars behind, setting our sights on the outskirts of town, the sparse pine forest next to the little beach. We drove with the windows open. There was the sound of soft leaves smeared under the tires. Big lights illuminated the jogging trails. At times I'd lay down in the backseat, carsick or drowsy from sugary Pepsi.

Some nights we moved no faster than a crawl. This made it possible to see the retirees in reflective vests and their unleashed, well-trained dogs who sat politely without moving when we drove by. Other nights we travelled way over the speed limit. The roads were empty and everything was soft: the ground, the leaf-filled, muddy ditches, even the tree trunks looked soft and I pictured them receiving us in a slow, rocking embrace in case Lan Pham were to lose control and send us skidding into the forest.

One evening we were stopped by the police. Lan Pham turned off the engine. Classical music on the radio. A burly man stepped out of his patrol car, the blue lights shining on his gleaming boots in the rear-view mirror.

The cop, a young man, smirked. He was cleanshaven and well-coiffed, with pale, clear eyes.

'Terrible weather tonight, Officer.'

Lan Pham and her reedy, boyish voice. It was as if something somehow gave way in the officer. He cleared his throat.

He looked me in the eye, then Má, one by one, his gaze sweeping over us, before wishing us a good evening.

Lan Pham was looking straight ahead, on alert, both hands on the wheel.

Had she scared him?

We skidded off.

Má stared in front of her. Her hands were in her lap. Lan Pham assured her again and again that it was fine, it was just a routine stop.

I lay down in the backseat. We drove homeward and someone turned off the radio.

NOT YET

I saw his longing at night. He turned in his sleep, everything was still revolving around Laura, she hadn't left us, not yet, I saw her whenever I looked at him and I knew, I could sense it, all of a sudden I had the realisation: nothing was better than resisting a temptation.

POEMS

After these drives Lan Pham liked to buy a bunch of magazines for her and Má to page through together. They would sit in the kitchen and someone would be ugly, someone was disgusting, someone was *so dear*. It was mostly white men: curly hair and moustaches; white, boyish, clean-shaven men, white, bare-chested men with veiny arms.

Sportsmen.

The pages turned with great frenzy. It didn't stop until Hieu came home.

Má proposed heading into the living room. Lan Pham brought the magazines and Má got on the sofa next to her. They looked through the ones they hadn't already got to.

When Hieu hung up his jacket Lan Pham started to speak in a loud voice. She had a *story*. It was something she'd been told by her cousins in Quy Nhơn, about a single dad who lived in a village outside the city. He spent every day complaining, enlisting the whole village in this activity, though what bothered him was something neither he nor the villagers had the power to fix. The problem was that his son was at the hospital. The father had gone to see him, the hospital was in the city, and the visit had ended with the father yelling at his son in a voice so loud that it echoed through the hospital corridors.

WHAT DID I DO WRONG?

The son didn't respond. The father turned to the doctor.

HE'S BEEN WRITING POEMS AND NOW HE'S ALL TWISTED!

HE LEFT HIS TAXI AND HIS FAMILY!

LEFT THEM HIGH AND DRY!

The son had lost his ability to speak and didn't say a word. Following this hospital visit the father had started to cause trouble back home in the village.

Lan Pham was imitating the shouting father, yelling from the sofa. Hieu was standing in the doorway to the kitchen, looking at the TV, which was off.

After his second hospital visit the father had stumbled around the village, still complaining. His son had been writing poems and now he was all twisted, he wasn't speaking at all, not even to his father, not a word... He had been writing poems...

Lan Pham was a good storyteller, she had an expressive voice and it was easy to follow her, but this time it was as if she wanted a fight. Some days it was obvious, she was ready to attack. It wasn't until Hieu left, slamming the door to our bedroom, that she stopped talking. I squinted at the living room window. It was one of the last evenings of autumn. If you sat perfectly still you could feel the warmth of the white sun's stinging rays in your face.

Poems!

ALSO ME

The sounds through the open window on a mild day. Accelerating cars: the tires screeched and they ran me over, also me they ran over.

LOVERET

It wasn't the first time we wondered about Hieu's whereabouts. Sometimes he stayed out after school, sometimes he'd be at Tobaksmagasinet, a community space where he played Tony Hawk with the other boys, or he'd be roaming the streets, which was what Má feared. Hours could go by. We were accustomed to not knowing. We went to bed as usual, but long past bedtime I heard Má make tea and sit down in the kitchen. She picked up her cup and put it back down on the table.

The morning after, a Saturday, she called Mrs Tuyet. Mrs Tuyet said that her daughter, who was in the year above Hieu, didn't recall seeing him the day before. At this Má took a deep breath and asked to speak directly to the daughter. She asked how the daughter was doing, said she hoped she was doing well in school, and asked if the daughter might have the number of any of Hieu's friends. Má was speaking in a strange tone – sing-song – that made her voice sound unusually inviting. Then she was silent. Mrs Tuyet's daughter was speaking. Má puckered her lips and tensed her jaws. Her cheeks were twitching. She shook her head, languidly and absentmindedly; she looked at her feet and I heard the sweet voice of the daughter from the receiver, she was talking and Má lowered the phone – Mrs Tuyet's daughter was speaking into the void with her sweet voice until Má interrupted her by hanging up.

We got the phone book and started to look through the pages. He'd been away for just one night.

Who was he spending time with these days?

How about calling Laura?

What was Laura's last name?

What were the first names of Laura's parents?

How about calling his teachers?

Who were his teachers? Would it affect his grades if they knew? She got the contact sheet for the school staff. Then she sat down, print-out in hand, staring at the phone.

How about calling Gunnel?

Gunnel?

Má got up and we went outside. It was pointless to keep looking through the phone book. Just a bunch of fluttering pages.

We stopped at the kiosk to buy cigarettes.

It was windy and the smoke blew into my face.

We went to the sports field.

We went to the beach. There was always someone at the beach.

We went to Tobaksmagasinet. A group of kids were smoking and drinking Red Bull outside. I entered the enormous brick building. At the Vietnamese New Year parties everything in there was decorated in dark red. Now: whitewashed brick walls, rugged columns from floor to ceiling, no chairs. I went to the second floor and the gaming rooms at the end of the hallway where they had Xbox and PlayStation and billiards and table tennis. Everyone was speaking Finnish. A poetry workshop was underway behind a closed door, it was its third year of running. The autumn programming.

Má was smoking next to the kids. She saw me come down the stairs. I shook my head and she shook her head.

She put a hand to her eyes. She took my hand and we walked.

It was one of those aimless, furious walks.

We went to the vocational school and back to the town centre, via the swimming pool and the football stadium. We walked past the squat rentals on the esplanade by the canal. Hot air came billowing from the laundry rooms in the basements, snaking out through small, barred windows. Má smoked an entire pack, finishing the last one while we walked up hilly Loveret, a street lined by yellow multi-story buildings with big windows and chandeliers in the stairwells.

Cigarette smoke, laundry detergent.

Old heather.

Piles of apples.

We kept our eyes out.

Strollers, old couples, dogs. Strangers' eyes everywhere. They lingered, looked us up and down and then up again, glared like they couldn't stop themselves. I came closer to Má, I let her take my arm and we walked this way for a brief while – my arm linked with hers – until she let go.

We were almost home, we walked around the block.

We were both still up when Hieu came home. He said nothing, he simply passed us on his way to the bedroom, but when Má asked, he replied immediately. He said he'd been at his girlfriend's.

What girlfriend?

That night, when Hieu was back in bed, the images returned, without forewarning. It was the first summer. An air freshener dangled in the rear-view mirror. The green landscape flickered outside. They'd dropped me off and then they left. I'd spent a week at Lan Pham's girlfriend's in the tall building at the end of Rådhusgatan. A full week – while they were out in the forest, Má, Hieu, Lan Pham, and Auntie Tei Tei.

That's how it all started. I was too young for the forest and I had missed everything: all the things they saw, all the things they heard.

I FEEL STRONG

The windshield wipers clean the fog from the window. Stefan's car is stately. A large vehicle. That's what Má thinks as she gets comfortable, adjusts the seat and mirrors. The driver sits high above the road.

It's the middle of summer.

She's a practiced driver, but handling someone else's car is a special responsibility, and there's trouble already in the first curve. The steering is slow to respond and the car ends up almost wholly in the wrong lane. She's forced to take her hand from the gear and use all her strength, both hands, to set it right again. Hieu yelps and giggles loudly.

Auntie Tei Tei looks indifferent; not angry, not sad, not amused. She keeps this expression the entire drive, aside from at one point when she catches herself thinking about herself. Here she smiles, but nobody notices – it's a very brief smile. She smiles at how silly the thought was, but above all she smiles because the thought was about her. The thought: *I feel strong*.

They've squeezed into the front seat, all of them. Side by side: Má, Lan Pham, Hieu, and Auntie Tei Tei.

Má lights a cigarette; Auntie Tei Tei asks her to roll down the window. After two drags Auntie Tei Tei tears the Wonder Tree from the mirror and flings it out the window. Má flinches. That's not like Auntie Tei Tei. But then she wonders: What is

Auntie Tei Tei like, anyway? It's their first group project in the new country and the second time they're in the same car. She assumed that Auntie Tei Tei wanted to air out the smoke; she'd never have thought she'd chuck the Wonder Tree...

Hieu wakes up. He looks out the window and squints, sharpening his gaze. It doesn't take long to get to the small, unfamiliar locality where Gunnel brought them a week earlier. Turning onto the backroads it's as if they've entered a new continent. The vegetation changes in an instant, there's green everywhere they look and the forest sways like a billowing sea around them. The lulling smoothness of the asphalt has dissolved and turned into gravel. A long stretch of this foreign terrain, the car vibrating and rocking Má into a new rhythm. Her pulse slows. When they shout at her it's as if she's been numb. She pulls off and they get out. The door handles, which were dewy when they started, are dry and warm. It's a brilliant afternoon.

Hieu laughs wildly and bounds over to a trail he's spotted.

Má skips over the ditch and cautiously taps the ground with her foot.

Dry.

She walks farther in between the trees. Then she stops, shuts her eyes, breathing as slowly and deeply as she can. The air is so different here, you can almost taste it. She tries to remember what Gunnel showed and explained. Crouching, she sees a berry and then a few more in the vicinity of the first. She'd like to be able to view the world through a thermal camera that shows only the berries and nothing else. Lan Pham yells from the other side of the road, calling for Má who shouts back.

> Lan Pham: *What do you think?*
> Má: *I'm not sure.*

Auntie Tei Tei sticks close to the ditch. She squats cautiously to smell the young, white flowers whose buds have just bloomed. She breathes in through her nose, producing a sharp, whining sound. Nobody hears it. Not even Hieu who is nearby. Nor does anybody hear her mumble quietly to herself: *We'll keep driving, we'll keep driving.*

They keep driving and they stop three times in places that are indistinguishable from each other: purple and blue here and there but nowhere near as lush as the place Gunnel took them on that first excursion. Their spirits remain high but the excitement that reigned when they first took off has waned. They're back in the car, the road winding endlessly before them. Dusk is falling. They're wasting time.

They're wasting time; Má is about to give up. She would never say it out loud but she's started to wonder if it's just a naïve dream that they got obsessed with and would do best to drop. Maybe they should forget about the whole thing... They've already asked Gunnel to help them get a vendor permit from the local government. Má frowns at the impenetrable, leafy landscape. She's in the midst of it.

That's when Auntie Tei Tei pipes up. Without hesitation, impatient, almost irritated: *Here, stop right here*. Má breaks, unfastens her seatbelt, opens the door, and springs out, all in one fluid motion. She taps the ground with her foot.

In the moment prior, in between when Auntie Tei Tei ordered Má to brake and when Má braked, they were all asking themselves — even Hieu wondered — how can Auntie Tei Tei be that confident?

They get out at a section of the forest that looks identical to the other spots, but something is different. Everyone gets out, even Lan Pham; newly awake, a little sluggish. It might just be the light, the sky that's closed, but something is different. Má taps a foot on the ground.

It's damp.

MY FIRST LONGING

Blue light on the blinds. Five days had passed since Hieu finally came home. Now there was a police officer at the door: an oddly calm, tall, and gangly officer, kind of pale and with a soft and easy voice.

No sirens.

He spoke clearly. Slowly and at just the right pitch, to make sure we understood. Still, it was barely audible. A nearly anaesthetizing impression.

Má understood him and all the colour drained from her face.

We were able to look through the window as Hieu followed the officer to the patrol car. A colleague opened the back door. Hieu bent to get in, and they left.

That night Má came to me when I was at my desk with my history book. A spread about the Viking era. I was thinking about Laura, a trembling sort of longing. Má leaned over my shoulder, held me close and pressed her cold face to mine.

I thought about Laura. This was my first longing. It was clear to me that nothing could have stopped me – if she'd been there I would have leapt up and ran to her.

Since Hieu revealed that he'd been sleeping at his new girlfriend's he hadn't said another word.

SWOLLEN

Friday slipped into Saturday. Má was composed. She walked around with the duster and used it everywhere she could reach. She cleaned the TV with a moist rag.

She wiped the coffee table.

The shelves. The windowsill.

She emptied the bucket of dirty water.

We spent all day cleaning.

I helped her in the kitchen. She wiped the inside of the microwave and I was at the sink with the heavy glass turntable, which constantly risked slipping out of my hands. Later, when it was time for dinner, we premiered the newly shining microwave by heating a pizza for each of us. We ate in the sofa in front of the crisp images of the TV. The news: clamour on the square, the president.

Hieu would be kept overnight. That's what they said when they called: they would hold him overnight, just one night. After the call Má stayed near the phone, holding her hand on the receiver as if waiting for another call.

How could it take 24 hours?

What kinds of questions were they asking him?

She ambled around and spoke repetitively and incessantly to herself.

She repeated the officer's words in her odd Swedish.

Friday or Saturday with Má in the clean apartment. No smell of sweat, nobody who kept opening and closing doors. That night Lan Pham appeared in my dream, a dream that replayed several times, a repetition of an image of Hieu and Lan Pham: Hieu on his bike, Lan Pham on her moped. Lan Pham drives her moped on a narrow asphalt trail, surrounded by tiny trees. It's a forest, or perhaps a densely planted park. Hieu and I are far behind, he's biking and I'm on his rear rack with my head leaned to the side and my arms tightly clasped around his waist. Lan Pham is fast, so fast she's almost out of sight, she's a vanishing spot on the horizon, barely visible, but her voice is recognisable, that thin voice that overlays everything like a crystalline membrane. Lan Pham in front of us on her gleaming red moped: now and then she turns around and exclaims something, speaking with a striking urgency – really using her whole body to say it – but it's impossible to hear. Hieu is pedalling like crazy and my hold of his waist hardens, a reflexive tightening, and as my grasp hardens I realise that we're the same height, that my body is as big as his, that it's swollen, that my arms are as strong and hairy as his. It is then, accompanied by Lan Pham's barely audible, anxious sounds, that I wake up.

WHAT THE OFFICER SAID

'I'm here because we've received a report from a girl in Oxhamns alleging that your son hit her. She was taken to the hospital and wasn't discharged until yesterday.'

AS IF UNDER WATER

Lan Pham is riding her moped and now and then she turns around, her mouth is a perfect circle and her speech is muffled, inaudible, as if under water.

TOKYO STORY

Má was in a long, faltering phone conversation. No more than an hour later Mr Tèo rang the doorbell. They had been talking about Hieu.

I snuck up and got on my tiptoes, my fingers softly bent against the door so I could observe Mr Tèo through the peephole. Now he and I were watching each other and he didn't know. He was waiting. He was dressed in a grey hat. His thin, black hair hung over the tall forehead. When he rang the doorbell again I cupped my hands over my ears. He must have heard me by now, the way I inadvertently scraped against the door, but he stayed there for a good long while, gazing straight ahead, silent and immobile. Not a peep from Má from inside the apartment.

Eventually he left. Má cautiously lifted the curtain, and we watched him cross the yard. Later I went out to buy some milk and discovered the bag hanging on the door handle. It was a brown paper bag with a letter in it – a slim, white envelope with Má's name on it and a paper roll held together by a wide rubbed band. I hung the bag on the inside of the door and went to the store. It wasn't until a few days later, when Hieu was back home again, that I noticed the change in Má's bedroom. By the foot of the bed, next to the unframed mirror on the otherwise bare wall, there was now a big poster in matte, milky colours showing the father and daughter in *Tokyo Story*, with the title printed in white on a dark-red background. It was elegant, almost irresistible, the way the morning sun was cast across the image, from the right-side corner down the left, over the father's wooden sandals.

I TRAVELLED IN THE LIGHT

Hieu was sleeping at home again. Only two days had passed since the police came, but everything was back to normal. Má had stayed home from work all day. She didn't care, she said, the boss could fire her if he liked, she'd get her severance either way. He could fire her, but there was no reason to do that since there were tons of people ready to cover if she needed time off. Jakobstad teemed, it was often said, with unemployed Vietnamese.

Sometimes I could sense it already in the afternoon: a silvery sheen around the torn clouds, an odd gleam over the tree in the yard. Later, while I waited to fall asleep, it would spread all over my field of vision and I could see my dreams even before they were dreamed. I was tossed between the images, memories that weren't my own. I travelled in the light.

AUNTIE TEI TEI'S
NOCTURNAL MOVEMENTS

The cargo area is bare. The tool boxes, the wooden scaffolding, the plywood, the work clothes — they've brought everything that belongs to Gunnel and her husband down to the basement, where it is now neatly stacked along the wall. Auntie Tei Tei unfolds the soft mattresses and hurries to get outside in the fresh air. Má lays down to rest. She shuts her eyes, it's almost time to sleep, but her heart is racing, rays shoot from her chest and tap against her eyelids, a pulse that brightens with every beat until she is finally forced to open her eyes.

She looks around. The sun has set but you can still see everything. It's spacious for a car. Two totes that contain clothes; bags with food. The stack of empty pails. The grey-brown backroad past her feet, the already mosquito-bitten feet that she rubs against each other. She tilts her head to the side and shuts her eyes only to slowly open them again. She spots a soaring, swaying figure in the midst of the absolute green. It moves strangely, like an enormous butterfly; a careless, odd butterfly that floats farther and farther away. Auntie Tei Tei and her purple cover jacket. Má smiles at this—at Auntie Tei Tei and the way she moves. She knows, too, that Hieu is in the forest. She can't hear him, but she knows he's there, and she knows what he sees as he darts through the blueberry brambles. She knows what it looks like because she's seen it herself, and that vision is what's made her go take a rest. Her careening heart has not yet settled. She shuts her eyes and pictures what Hieu sees: the soft blueberry brambles – billowing and brightening – and this, finally, forces her to open her eyes. She shuts them again, rolls over. She'll start working soon. But right now she's resting.

Later, after many hours of work and a drawn-out dusk, they all lay down to sleep. Má has attached a small flashlight – the size of a thumb – to the ceiling of the van's hold, and now it dangles from the hook, a gentle glow. *What a day*. That's what she'd like to say, loudly, but she doesn't. Lan Pham is curled up in her sleeping bag by the wall, already asleep, and Auntie Tei Tei has taken the front, the folded seats. Hieu's spot is in the centre of the floor in the back, he has his own little mattress. His legs and arms are sprawled, he's entirely uncontained. Má covers him with the blanket. He's on his back, making a whistling sound as he breathes through his nose. She looks at him, listening: is that a whimper? It's as if it is to avoid getting stuck in this listening that she finally turns off the light and gets into her sleeping bag. What a day. They've been working all day and all night and they'll keep going tomorrow. The sounds in the hold of the van: Hieu's breathing, sleeping bags rustling. Intermittent wind and the whooshing of tree tops, a barely audible soughing that rocks them into the night. Wing flaps, slowly fading. A distant hoot, maybe from an owl. These are the sounds she listens to. It doesn't take long, after a while you get used to the darkness, your vision improves. Through the window that separates the hold from the front seat she perceives Auntie Tei Tei's nocturnal movements: Auntie Tei Tei sits up, turns, stops, waits.

Right before Má falls asleep she hears the passenger door close. It's a protracted closing, so careful and quiet that you don't actually hear the door shut—at first you hear the forest's low whooshing, and then you don't.

UP

Mikael lived in one of the weird housing expo buildings. They lined the slithering concrete street, which was so narrow that cars could barely pass each other. His sister had moved abroad, and he lived with his mum and dad who worked every day from morning to evening. It was a two-story house with red rafters and big glass windows looking onto the backyard. Next door was a playground with big trees and a pond where goldfish swam in the summer. The neighbourhood was called Europa. After school Atdhe, Mikael, and I biked to the weird house and played FIFA 2000 on Mikael's dad's computer. Some days we played table tennis in the shed off the driveway. They had squeezed in a small table among the garden furniture and tools. Atdhe held the racquet the way he'd seen Chinese players do on TV.

One day we turned on the big TV in the living room. It was showing a rerun from 1997, when Finland played Hungary in Helsinki. Finland scored an own goal in the final minutes of the game, and the ref called it soon thereafter. It was raining. The sports caster was speaking Finnish. It sounded as if he was crying.

Finns and football...

We turned the TV off and went to Mikael's dad's home office to play FIFA.

All of us had favourite teams. Atdhe's was France. Mikael liked Argentina. Sometimes I chose Nigeria and they rolled their eyes. It was an unusual choice which, since it wasn't a top team, had the effect of making their wins over me less valuable.

I chose Nigeria because of Jay-Jay Okocha, the world's best dribbler. I repeatedly tried to accomplish his signature feint: the Okocha Stepover, which he'd used to humiliate Denmark's back line in the world championships. I almost didn't care about winning the game as long as I got the dribbling right.

When Mikael and Atdhe played each other I entertained myself by trying to provoke them, or, put another way, by making them emotionally activated. At one point I stumbled on an unusual phrase that set the room on fire: when Atdhe broke out of the pack with Emmanuel Petit—not a particularly speedy guy—I pressed Mikael to block him *up*. This put us in a brand-new mood. We laughed riotously. We raised our voices and talked over each other, we finished each other's sentences. From there on, our way of talking to each other had a certain excitement to it. We spent the rest of the day and several months afterwards experimenting with this new *up*.

If you were free, one on one with the goalie, all you had to do was smack it up.

If the rival team's forward was free you could, once again, block him up.

If the ref seemed partial someone must have paid him up.

If you were facing a strong wall of defenders and couldn't pass the ball, well, you might try to feint them up.

And so on, and so on.

Mikael and Atdhe played until they were sweaty, they snarled and cursed. I psyched them up. It was dizzying, the way you could achieve something so great simply by uttering a few words.

I WAS HAPPY

The birds were sitting on the farthest end of the branches, their feathers mottled in blue and yellow. I caressed Má's unwashed hair. She slowly lifted her head and wiped her eyes with the sleeve of her sweater. She got up and went to her bedroom. Rustling sheets. I stayed put and watched the beautiful birds.

Blue tits.

Where was Hieu?

A long afternoon. Nothing happened. Má came out of the bedroom and said Hieu's name. She was speaking to me but she used his name. At times it was as if she was doing by trying: if she wanted to speak to Hieu she'd say my name first and then his, and if she had something she wanted to say to me she might say his name first and then mine.

That evening our plan was to walk over to Lan Pham's. Má strode into the street. It was a cloudless, pleasant Sunday and we had dressed up, as if going to church: Má in black tights and a long, green dress, and me in a pale blue shirt and a thin, grey cotton cardigan. Lan Pham lived in Skutnäs and we seemed to be in a hurry. Má held my hand in a tight grip, her face turned away. I watched her closely.

The movements of the hipbone, her twitchy arms when she pressed my hand.

A sweat stain slowly bloomed between her shoulder blades.

Her hair was arranged in a bun that looked like it might collapse at any moment.

Hollyhocks and groups of smoking teens. The benches outside the cemetery were occupied by old men and women who had their sleeves rolled up and their eyes closed to the sun, faces like dinner plates lined up like that, motionless in the sunshine.

This was a street I'd biked on multiple times. Vestersundsby School was at the end, with an ice hockey rink and a grass field. I could almost hear the yelling and laughter, the wolf whistles.

We were in a hurry, Má and me.

I came to think of Atdhe and Juri and Besnik and Jürgen. I thought of them and the passing sequences on the Vestersundsby field: those rare moments of free, very intensive playing, when swarms of insects buzzed around us, mosquitoes and bugs making every single one of us, even the laziest and most unwilling player, reluctant to stand still. This produced ever-shifting formations of players that moved as if in waves, back and forth at an incomprehensible speed. The roles dissolved and we took each other's positions, threw ourselves on the ball, snorted and yelled. The game was characterised by an unusually permissive commitment: even if you failed it was a sign of ambition that you'd tried something difficult.

Just before the streetscape changed into wooden villas we turned down a gravel road that led to the high rise where Lan Pham lived. Má took a breath. She let go of my hand and found her lipstick, opened the cap.

The stairwell had no decorations whatsoever, the entrance was lit by something resembling a bedside lamp and there was a smell of sour milk in the air. On the landing between the second and third floor I closed my eyes. I saw it again, the passing sequences, they came back to me like translucent, moving photographs. We were outside Lan Pham's door on the third floor and my eyes were still closed. I saw my and Juri's one-two pass, I saw my feint kick and the kick that immediately followed, the tufts in the cut grass, the neon vests... Má rang the doorbell. She gave herself a nervous kind of smile, which increased in wattage when the door slowly opened. It was dead silent in the stairwell and Má put out her hand and cautiously opened the door a little more. Lan Pham had bags under her eyes. She turned and walked in, waving her hand at us.

I haven't cleaned.

She was dressed in a turquoise bathrobe and leather trousers. We sat down in the living room. There were glasses and plastic cups and empty cans everywhere and she started tidying, instructing us to relax while she made coffee.

Family photos, bills, advertising leaflets, the local newspaper... Beige sheets on the bed. This was an ordinary apartment, nothing special, it looked more or less like ours, even the kitchen; she had lots of cups and accessories related to coffee but other than that it was unremarkable. Except for the balcony. An incredible sight: I froze in the doorway when we went outside with the cups and saucers. Lan Pham's garden was incredible: a swell of flowers in flashy colours, tall climbing plants with thick trunks, chili bushes and citrus trees. You lost yourself out there, sank and got swallowed by all the colours.

We squeezed in around the wooden table that barely fit the coffee set. They had coffee and I had rooibos, a beverage *rich in antioxidants*—Lan Pham had made a pot just for me and I drank cup after cup of the sweet drink. At one point Má's hand moved in the direction of an enormous red, speckled flower. She came close, touched it with exaggerated care.

Dusk was already approaching. Má moved to the back

balcony wall where she now crossed her legs and lit a cigarette. Lan Pham complained about the view, that there was nothing to see; *but*—and she leaned over the railing and pointed at the corner, the street behind the house—*from here, though!*

She pointed at an old couple and their two dogs.

Really gross dogs… Hahahaha!

Her laughter echoed over the street. The dog owners looked up and kept walking with brisk steps. Má gazed at the sky and laughed quietly. I finished my rooibos and now I felt it, it was palpable: the whole thing was so humorous.

Lan Pham went inside to finish cleaning. Má and I stayed behind in the warm, darkening summer night. We looked at the treetops in the distance, the aspens lining the cemetery, the neighbouring buildings with their identical entrances, the bike shed, the grass, the swing set. I watched Lan Pham through the window. She got the vacuum cleaner and plugged it in. She'd discarded the robe and was walking around in a bra and tight black leather trousers. Her torso exposed: birth marks and bare, tanned shoulders. Má took the chance to smoke, she took Lan Pham's cigarettes from next to the ashtray and smoked three in quick sequence.

Lan Pham had finished cleaning.

She was sitting in an armchair and gestured for us to come inside.

Má and I moved to the sofa.

They started talking about Hieu. That's how it all started.

Me: looking through some magazine.

Má: following three hastily smoked cigarettes.

Lan Pham: in leather trousers.

Má was, initially, composed.

It was when she took a folded piece of paper from her pocket and asked Lan Pham to translate a couple of sentences for her that everything stopped. The envelope had the police seal on it. Lan Pham unfolded the piece of paper. She rolled her eyes. She couldn't quite understand why she was being asked to translate those sentences. She asked why Má didn't get one of us – Hieu or me – do it.

This one here can do it! Why do you look so pitiful?

She pointed at me with her red nail.

Má replied, still in a soft voice, that I was too young for that, and it was then, before Má had time to finish the sentence, that Lan Pham launched into a set of impertinent questions.

Who do you think I am?

and:

Am I working right now? Do I look like an interpreter? Does this look like my uniform?

I went outside and joined the flowers on the balcony.

Inside the apartment they raised their voices.

I lay down on the narrow bench and squinted. The sunflowers towered against the grey sky, dark circles that slowly pulsed in and out of their own contours. Sounds from the kids at the playground down the street. Cars.

Má raised her voice. She accused Lan Pham of having *behaved badly*. It was Lan Pham's fault that Hieu hit that girl.

Lan Pham had been unusually still and quiet throughout our visit – something indifferent in the way she moved – but when Má made this claim about Hieu, saying that Lan Pham bore the guilt of what Hieu had done, she put down her coffee mug with a slam. She got up. She yelled. She gesticulated. She asked if it was her fault that Má had nursed Hieu until he was four, too.

Back and forth. They kept going.

The whole thing ended with Lan Pham lecturing Má to choose her words carefully, saying that she couldn't say whatever she wanted just because she was struggling right now, that it was preposterous of Má to put all of it on her. A long silence followed. I didn't move from the balcony bench. The flowers' bright colours. It was as if they were vibrating with heat, despite the chill in the air.

What had Lan Pham done?

How could it be her fault?

Later, when I turned around and looked through the window, the sofa was empty. Both of them were in the armchair, snuggled up to each other, Lan Pham and Má, sort of on top of each other, embracing, Má with one hand cupped over Lan Pham's shoulder. Did they have their eyes closed? I went inside with the coffee set, all the way to the kitchen, my eyes on the clattering porcelain.

Lan Pham had done a truly efficient job cleaning the place. She even vacuumed the hall, returned her shoes to the rack. She'd put away all the clutter, done the dishes, folded the tablecloths.

It was dark outside.

Má and Lan Pham got out of the armchair and came to me in the hall. We put our shoes on, brief hugs, and then Má and I walked down the stairs.

We started walking down the street, very slowly – a restrained stroll – and then we heard running steps behind us. We turned around and there she was, in a bathrobe and slippers, Má flung her arms around her. All of us were lightly dressed, we were standing in the middle of the street in our thin, fluttering garments: me in a shirt, Má in a dress, Lan

Pham in a bathrobe. There was not a soul around. We were standing close to each other, Má and Lan Pham in each other's arms. Má's breathing was rapid and shallow, she was about to say something, and then, when she spoke, she looked right into my eyes, but it was as if she was speaking to someone else, because what she said was incomprehensible.

I thought about my husband... We were out on a walk with the kids... We stopped at the cotton trees... We watched them sleep... I was happy...

Viewed from the street Lan Pham's incredible balcony looked like all the other balconies. A twig or two that stretched past the railing, a flash of colour between the laths. Lan Pham asked if we didn't want to come back up, she could make us tea – but it was too late, we should have left ages ago; I had school and so did Hieu.

NO COFFEE

We stood there on the empty street and Má had slipped her hands inside Lan Pham's robe. Beneath the blue silk cloth her fingers dug into Lan Pham's shoulder blades.

I thought about my husband...We were out on a walk with the kids...We stopped at the cotton trees...We watched them sleep...I was happy...

I was so close I could hear them breathe.

They embraced on the street, and we went home. There was silence after that. Lan Pham didn't get in touch again. Má moved Lan Pham's coffee set to the back of the cupboard. Má had whispered in Lan Pham's ear and I'd heard everything she said but after that: no more rides in her Fiat, no spontaneous visits, no coffee. She had bumped into Hieu and his friend outside Prisma. She'd given them a primer on how to behave around girls, she'd told them to be direct.

I started to picture Lan Pham in the forest. Lan Pham in the forest: silent, and, believe it or not, entirely without colour.

GLUT

The first real workday. They stay close to one another. Hieu has his own pail, a child-sized version that he fills up fast, even before the first eating break. He sprints to the van. He proceeds without asking, he walks up to the big, empty plastic buckets and carefully tips in the first load of berries, blue on white, watching them just barely cover the bottom. Then he jumps out of the van, pulling the side door shut as he lands on the gravel with a thud. Má, Lan Pham, and Auntie Tei Tei are all in sight, vanishingly small dots in the unbelievably bright landscape.

Má puts down her pail and berry harvester. Hands now free, she kills the mosquitoes on her arms one by one. She regrets her choice of clothing. She's wearing a long, pleated skirt and tights that don't stop any bugs. She did bring actual work trousers; they're in her backpack in the car and nobody would notice if she went to change, everyone is occupied, deeply focused, but she hesitates, delays, crouches. The blueberry brambles are towering and big from this vantage point. Close up she looks at the leaves which are turned toward the sun and shimmer in red and yellow. The sight reminds her of clementine trees. She puts her fingers around one of the berries, a superb specimen – a perfectly spherical, smooth surface – and then puts it in her mouth, crushes it between her teeth, letting it slowly melt on her tongue. She stays like that, squatting, apparently distracted.

It's the racing heart.

Blueberry brambles. Violet, dark, and paling berries.

There's Hieu. There's Lan Pham. At even intervals one of them will glance her way. She's thinking that she needs to let herself be carried away by the work if this is going to lead to anything. Blinded by the sun – it's red already, it sifts through the unfamiliar-looking trees from high in the sky – Má decides to change.

It turns out that they're too big, the work trousers. Má ties them with a ribbon in the waist and folds the hems, folds them repeatedly; they keep falling and dragging and getting stuck in the thorny underbrush of the pine forest.

Lan Pham has heard that this year the blueberry brambles flowered already in May, that the spring was so reliably warm that they were spared the night frost. A warm spring, a couple of mild nights in May, and now all of this... How did it come to pass? Lan Pham can't quite figure it out. It doesn't make sense, and actually it's pretty frustrating to her, not knowing. What exactly are they dealing with here? Could a few mild nights in May really have brought them all of this? A few mild nights in May... She searches across linguistic borders. There's no better word, not any she can think of right now: what they're facing is a 'glut', a 'glutting'.

Finally, wearing her work trousers, Má can move with ease. They're green, with deep pockets. She tries to locate the others, she spots Lan Pham and when she compares their clothes she realises that everyone, including Auntie Tei Tei and Hieu, are wearing long trousers and padded jackets: an observation that leads to a conclusion. They share a uniform. This concept of a uniform – it's hilarious to her. Now unencumbered, she bends and sweeps her berry harvester and quickly fills her pail to the brim. She's in flow, she barely needs to look.

Hieu traverses the boggy ground. He keeps an eye out for water pools, there are lots of them, he knows this because he just encountered one. In fact he almost stepped in it, almost, it was hidden, shallow and obscured thanks to the shadows cast by the trees bent over the grey water. The surface was so still you could see your own reflection in it. He found it without looking. The reflection: his face between the trunks, the grey lustre. Now he's looking. It makes it easier, he thinks, finding is easier when you're looking.

BIOLOGY CLASS

Just as some were too scared to walk near the deep pool in the swimming hall, there were a few of us who were afraid of the forest. In orienteering you could run – there was a map, you wore trainers, and the whole thing could be viewed as a game. In biology class we stood in a semi-circle, with Malin going on and on about this and that, saying we'd learn to distinguish species by scent and flavour, the way they looked in fall, winter, spring, and summer. The fear wasn't acute. Lockanberget – a big boulder – the firs in the forest by the harbour… Innumerable excursions had made the forest a familiar place. I fixed my gaze on the lamps – unlit – on top of the columns that lined the running trail. Malin regularly requested our attention. 'Hey guys' and 'look here' and 'listen up'. It was hard to follow her commands.

Malin, next to a tree stump: growth rings.

Malin, next to a fallen fir: windthrow.

Malin, squatting by an ant hill: queens.

We looked around, me and a few others, beset by some kind of compulsive restlessness.

The whole class walked back together. At the traffic lights I found myself next to Malin. The sky was turning grey. She turned to look at me and asked if I might be interested in joining Kvarken's Forest School. She mentioned some kind of spring excursion and an overnight camping trip. Since I didn't know if she was serious or not I responded with a friendly smile, the kind of smile that could mean anything.

MALIN'S TIRADE

Okay, everybody... So here we are... Why don't we start by... There's something I want you to keep in mind... You know, we might think we know everything, but then it turns out that we don't... And one subject people often have a lot of thoughts about is animals, and insects... Plants, too... For sure... But we'll stick to animals and insects for now... I know that many of you have pets at home... Dogs and cats... Rabbits... Parrots... Right... Hamsters... And you might think – actually let's use me as an example here – with our dog, sometimes I wonder... Like... What is he thinking about? Yeah, sometimes... You know... When we have eye contact and stuff... On the sofa... But now that we're here... That bird for example... It's a house sparrow, probably... You can't help but wonder... What's it thinking about? Why is it looking around like that? Well, okay... I said we'd focus on animals and insects, and the reason we've stopped here today is actually because I planned to talk about an insect not everyone might be familiar with... That insect is the tick... For those of you who don't know what a tick looks like I brought one in a jar... You can take a look later... In any case, the tick is an arachnid... I won't dwell on its life cycle but it's the usual: larva, nymph, adult, male, female... You know the drill... You're familiar with all that... You might have found a tick on your pet... Or even on yourselves! And that is because ticks have to suck blood from mammals and birds in order to propagate... And in so doing they can spread disease... It's not too uncommon, some people get pretty serious brain injuries... But that's not what we're here to talk about today... Like I said earlier... This thing about not knowing, or thinking that you know when you don't... And so today, if we home in on the tick here... It's been exhaustively studied... In fact, when I lived in Germany, that's what we were doing... Let's take my dogs as an example again... Of course it's easy to think that you love each other when the dog is in your arms and you're asleep in bed and... Yeah... It's cosy... You love your dog and the dog loves you back... But then there are times when you might think... You know... Maybe all the dog cares about is that you give it food... That's all it wants... Well, that's just life... Anyway, when I was working in Germany we were studying ticks... And specifically we were trying to understand... Maybe not what it was thinking since it's probably not really thinking much at all... But rather, what does it want... Or: what compels it to do the things it does... And we concluded that there are just three things a tick cares about in this world... Three things, no more... I'll list them for you, quickly... It's not complicated... The first thing it cares about is the scent of something called butyric acid... Which is something all mammals emanate... That's the first thing... The second is temperature... Which is to say, a specific temperature, it has to be that specific temperature... Or the tick doesn't care... And that temperature is 37 degrees Celsius... Which is the temperature of mammal blood... Which means that my dog and I... Our blood is the same temperature... The third thing the tick cares about is the skin type that mammals have... Superficial veins, and so on... And that's it! All they do in their tick life is wait... And if they're lucky they find a mammal to burrow their head in... After which they begin to suck the blood... This is also the beginning of the end for the tick... Since afterwards it falls off and lays its eggs... A whole lot of eggs... We counted 4,000-10,000 of them... And that's it as far as the tick goes... But what I want you to take from all this... How can I put it... So... My dog... If I as much as look at the leash he jumps up... And if I take the leash and go to the hall, that makes him all... Yeah... It's crazy... He wags his tail and jumps around and yelps... It's because he's learned to associate the leash with... The leash and walks, that's it... Those two go together... I want you to imagine a nice summer's day: the sun is shining, there's no wind, you're in the park, birds are chirping and bees are humming and there are pretty flowers all around... All the colours and the sounds... The tick doesn't know any of it... Doesn't care... All it does is wait for its three signs... You want to believe that it would at the very least enjoy the taste of warm blood... Or that it understands, at least, that it is blood that it's drinking... Since that's what it keeps waiting for... But in the lab we found that it would drink anything as long as the temperature was right... Remember, 37 degrees Celsius, we've talked about that before... Yuck... Awful... It will drink anything... So I don't know... It makes you wonder, you know... All those songs I've sung to my dog... What does he care... But I love him regardless... Oh well... There was one last thing I forgot to tell you... In Germany... In the lab we had there... When I started working there they had a tick they'd kept alive for 18 years... Do you understand... That's almost half of my life... For 18 years it had lived without any sustenance... Without anything at all... Just waiting...

It's exceptional... But there is something you can't help but ask... What kind of 18 years is that... Right... These are difficult questions... And what I'm trying to tell you here is... It's as if they're in their own little bubble... Do you see what I'm saying? Everyone has a bubble of their own, swooshing around... You can almost picture it... Soap bubbles whirling everywhere... Though of course soap bubbles do pop... Oh well... I just wanted to say... So... Butyric acid and all that... The life of a tick... If we return to picture that beautiful summer's day again... Maybe we're in a park... Or in a meadow... Bumble bees... Hares and birds... You might think that everyone exists in the same world, breathing the same air... But it turns out that's not the case... The tick only knows those three things I've been going on about... When it comes to the bumble bee, those things will be totally different... Humans too, come to think of it... We're also inside our own soap bubble... I guess that's it... That's what I want you to take away from this... Your own soap bubbles...

AGENT

We had stopped watching movies but the film poster was still in Má's room. Some mornings, when the low sun suffused the apartment with its thin light, the poster took on a new focus. It was shiny, as if Má had polished it overnight. *Tokyo Story*! I thought about the Vietnamese, how impatient they'd been at the doorbell downstairs, and the smile that spread over Má's lips every time she saw them through the window. I remembered the long nocturnal phone conversations where Má talked about actors and directors, about Japan and Vietnam, the bitter fate of various romantic couples.

These days we watched football instead. Music videos. There was shouting and laughter outside the window. One early night when the kids were chasing each other in the yard – zigzagging between the newly planted trees – I came to think of Jürgen and Besnik and Juri. I imagined them doing what all of us used to do at night: prowl around on our bikes, stopping at Korsgrundet where we'd do long shots across the centre circle – practicing straight, perfect long shots that landed smack in the middle of the receiver's chest. One day we noticed a man watching us from the side-lines. He was wearing a blazer and sat sideways on the rack of his bike with an elbow resting on the seat. He showed up several nights in a row, that same man. He never said a word, just sat there and smoked and watched us do our long shots. We joked that he was a foreign sports agent who'd come to scout Ostrobothnian talents, and even though we knew that none of us were good enough to be a pro, and though we knew that this man most likely was just a regular person — it was as if we made an extra effort on the days when he sat on his bike, smoking those cigarettes.

I didn't think about them because I missed them. I had left all that stuff behind. But I remembered Jürgen and Besnik and Juri as teammates. We'd been a team.

That night, as I sat by the window and thought of my old teammates, it was as if I knew what was about to happen: I knew that the images would come to me the moment I lay down to sleep, and I wouldn't be able to move at all, I wouldn't be able to fall asleep or get up. Surrounded by the night's numbing darkness I would lie in bed and think of them all in the forest, Hieu with blueberry juice smeared around his mouth, Auntie Tei Tei who never slept... An unbroken stream of images that came in spurts, like jellyfish in the water beneath my eyelids.

THE LEOPARD

One day Auntie Tei Tei shares that she's seen a leopard. It's the third day in the forest and her revelation, her story about having seen a leopard, takes everyone by surprise. It happens in the afternoon. They're taking a snack break and Auntie Tei Tei is sitting under a tall pine tree. She tears the plastic wrap off her baguette and looks embarrassed, fumbling with her arm in front of her face, tries to hide it. Finally they notice her impish look and the way her eyes are twitching. Má asks what's going on. At first she gets no response, Auntie Tei Tei just takes a mouthful of the baguette and concentrates on chewing. Lan Pham makes another attempt: speak, she says, but nothing happens. It's not until Hieu stumbles up and looks Auntie Tei Tei in the eye, asking what's *really* going on here, that she explains that this morning, just a few hours earlier and not at all far away – a stone's throw at most – she'd spotted a leopard. And not in passing, either – she'd observed it with great attention and it had looked back, looked her straight in the eye. Of course they all laugh upon hearing this, Má and Lan Pham, even Auntie Tei Tei laughs at what she's just told them. But not Hieu. He wants to know the distance, how much they were separated by, Auntie Tei Tei and the leopard, so he asks: *How close?* Auntie Tei Tei laughs.

There are no exotic animals in Finland. This is why they laugh.

They abandon the subject, they don't talk about it for the next several hours, but intermittently they hear Auntie Tei Tei laughing to herself. It's a pealing laughter that spreads, sort of slithers off and into the dense greenery in a way that might have been frightening were it not for the fact that it's Auntie Tei Tei's pealing laughter. They work together, but also independently, moving in their own circles. Every time Auntie Tei Tei laughs, Má and Lan Pham frown. Moreover, every time she laughs it's as if Hieu comes a little closer, a slow approach, Hieu's and Auntie Tei Tei's circles gradually nearing each other until they fully merge.

It's their third day in the forest. They work from morning till night. This lushness, an incredible, overwhelming abundance, means that they don't have to think about anything other than picking berries, and this day they pick like fanatics. Even in her frenzy Má can't stop her amazement at the amount of berries they've already gathered, in just two and a half days. Every time she goes to empty her pail in the van she can barely keep it together. It's that sight of the incredible piles of berries: the full vessels with lids on, stacked along the wall almost all the way to the ceiling. She decides to take her first nap of the day. She shuts the door and hopes — a prayer said silently as she pulls the side door closed — that the others won't show up and empty their pails while she's sleeping, that they'll come soon after she's woken up, to give her a chance to say something about the weather or perhaps comment on the abundance they're dealing with here. An absolute excess – *does it get any better than this?*, she'd like to ask, and then add that they've been lucky to find a place like this. She curls up, shuts her eyes, and falls asleep.

Auntie Tei Tei has worked for 24 hours straight without resting. This is something that happens to her with some regularity, but she knows others would find it strange, it's not something you can share with others just like that. So she keeps it to herself. She understands that she should probably keep most things to herself, it's better for everyone that way, and now she regrets having told them about the leopard. She wasn't able to stop herself and it's not like her, she thinks, to expose herself like that. She's not the type of person who, so to speak, spills over.

Hieu is hungry. The baguettes they've been eating since they arrived in the woods... It's all he'd ever wish for, you might even say it's his favourite food. He likes them best this way: when they've had the chance to sit for a while and the crust has hardened into a shell that crumbles at the first bite. He thinks about the hard bread, the juicy cucumber, the sour carrots and cabbage, the rubbery meat; he thinks about the exquisite sticky paste at the centre of the bread, which he's always considered part of the bread itself, an aspect of the bread's quality. But now as he recalls his most recent baguette, the one he ate sitting between the trees, he realises: it's the pâté that does it. He remembers how Má hurried with the ingredients in a plastic bowl the day before they left – pork liver and eggs and milk – using an immersion blender to make a paste. It took no more than a few seconds, and the result didn't look very good, actually. A green-brown paste reminiscent of vomit. But on a baguette – spread inside a crispy bread... These baguettes are his favourite food, and he tries to keep that in mind. Something doesn't feel quite right, however, and it's hard to ignore. In fact, he's tired of chewing – that's what it's all about, he's so tired of chewing. The berries they're picking, now he's started to swallow them whole. He can taste the flavour regardless, it's in the peel, he can tell from the colour what they taste like and so he swallows them whole. Inescapable thoughts, he must endure them, he knows there's nothing he can do about it, he knows not to complain. Still, he can't help but long for something different than the hardened, exquisite bread.

PRADA

Hieu and Má came home from the city administration office, where they had met with Hieu's case manager about the community service he'd been sentenced to. They didn't stop talking about the meeting; Hieu spent all evening trying to explain to Má what to expect in the time to come. Community service. A total of fifty hours spread out over three months. He was going to work – where exactly wasn't clear – various sorts of activities, it could be just about anything. Cleaning, baking... He would report to Jesper, his case manager, every week.

Various activities...

A few weeknights, but mostly during the weekend. During this time he could not, under any circumstances, fall behind in school.

It was all quite complicated. Má nodded, her eyes big.

They pored over those documents all night, their eyes boring through them, and Hieu did his best to translate and explain in Vietnamese. Má would need to digest the fact that he was going to have to work for fifty hours, entirely without pay. Before going to bed Hieu brought up something else, it was the final agenda item of their meeting. The case manager had mentioned it in passing, and when Hieu shared it with Má it sounded like he was presenting an attractive offer: in case he was interested he could go talk to a therapist in the city, entirely free of cost.

Má still knew lots of people. Now and then she'd talk on the phone with some girlfriend in Vietnam; when we were out in the city she'd often stop to chat with a Vietnamese acquaintance, and Gunnel still rang the doorbell sometimes for a brief visit. Má knew lots of people, but none of them made her light up like Lan Pham had done.

On some days it was as though Má dressed in whatever she happened to pick up. Other times, in preparation for special undertakings, she could spend hours putting together an outfit.

There was one day when she took particularly long. She brought her dresses and blouses and sweaters to the living room, left them on their hangers and fanned them out over the sofa. Then she went through them methodically, garment by garment, trying them on one by one and taking a look in the mirror. She walked back and forth, she looked over her shoulder, she came closer, she examined the clothes, examined her face; she came right up to the mirror and stared as if she was looking for something she'd only find through intent scrutiny. She hummed some kind of melody. When she'd finally decided she swept her arm over the sofa so that all the dresses and blouses and sweaters came together in a disorganised pile that she went and tossed on top of her bed.

She had chosen a thin, red dress, and the knit sweater she'd been gifted by Lan Pham.

Prada.

That's the word she said before hurrying out and down the stairs.

She was back an hour later.

Lan Pham wanted nothing to do with her.

Má had rung the doorbell and she heard someone moving about in there, but those first sounds were followed by silence, and nobody came to the door.

Má locked herself in her bedroom all night, and Hieu came home late.

He'd hit a girl...

It wasn't in Skolparken like the rumours said. Someone had heard Hieu curse at the girl and then they'd seen him pull her hair, dragging her towards the water fountain by the pond. This was the rumour, but later it emerged that the incident had occurred at her place. Her parents were away, and she and Hieu had planned to watch a movie. She was just home from a tennis lesson, they were going to eat a hamburger. He was going to sleep there one night, and one night turned into two. She was a girl from the neighbouring town, her big interest was tennis, she competed in the regional championships, they'd been dating for two weeks when he hit her and she'd been forced to call her parents at their hotel. They drove back home immediately, packed their bags in the middle of the night.

IMPORTS AND EXPORTS

Hieu and I were at the post office. We were there to pick up a package for Má and found ourselves in line behind a Vietnamese man who turned around and started to talk to us.

He asked what could be done...

Taking a number to wait in line...

He had no patience for such things.

I'm just here, thinking.

This made me want to ask what he was thinking about – something funny maybe, in order to distract himself, since he hated standing there with a number – but before I had a chance to ask he provided the answer himself. He told us he was thinking of *commerce: imports and exports.*

I had strange experiences in school, too. A little ways into the autumn there was an incident that stayed with me. It was one of those grey autumn days when you just want to finish your classes and go home, when stepping outside in the wind at breaktime is almost intolerable. I was sitting at my desk before class had started when Matti came up to me. He took a booklet from the jetted pocket of his blazer, he was leaning over me, supporting himself on the desk with one elbow. This booklet was laminated, not much bigger than his hand, with red flowers and green leaves scattered across the glossy cover. He opened to a page at the end of the book, and used two fingers, the pointer finger and the index finger, to trace down the entire page. It was a list of Finland's mammals.

'No monkeys... And no leopards, like I told you...'

He returned to the pulpit and started the class.
Did he have some kind of problem?
Why had he done that?

It was a question I wondered about for a long time, but I didn't get to ask. Ultimately the topic faded, this thing about monkeys and leopards. Was it something I'd said in class at some point, had I claimed there were monkeys in Finland?

Did I have some kind of problem?

NO DRAMA

Hieu spent the first weekends working at Tobaksmagasinet. A few weeks later he moved to Prisma, where he did inventory, but sometimes – in emergencies, he explained – they let him man the register. Not everyone realises this, but anyone working service in Jakobstad has to say everything, all the prices and greetings, in both Swedish and Finnish. One evening we were watching TV together and Hieu started to list prices, goods, and special offers mixed with thank you and hope to see you soon, all in one big jumble of Swedish and Finnish. It was as if he was reading some kind of poem on a stage, and Má began to laugh.

This was a time with no drama whatsoever. Hieu had to take care of both school and his sentence, and he often came home late, very tired, going straight to bed.

Má had picked herself up and was back at work.

The days passed – Má went to work, Hieu went to school – and nothing seemed to be happening. Was it boredom that led me to think of them out in the forest? I was drawn to them, the images, I let myself be swallowed up by them. Hieu and Má and Lan Pham and Auntie Tei Tei, bending over the blueberry bushes in silence.

HIEU HAS A BRILLIANT IDEA

They're consumed by their work in the forest, truly consumed at this point – that's what Má is thinking as she stands there in the midst of the brambles, now and then killing a mosquito that lands on her neck or throat. The market is in a few days and she's planned it all out. She's talked to Gunnel about the vending permits, the cheaper tables and the more expensive tables in central spots where lots of people pass through. The autumn market takes over the entire pedestrian street with food and candy, knick-knacks and homemade oddities. She's talked to Gunnel about the different phases of the market, the way the crowd ebbs and flows, at what point it's empty and at what point there's a rush, at what point they should make sure to staff their table fully to avoid queues. They've talked about every conceivable detail, even the weather.

Má has made her calculations: she's crunched the numbers, she's shared the information. She gets carried away easily, and she actually likes the idea of queues – they've all talked about avoiding queues, but to her they're hopeful, a sign of something. They create – what's the word – excitement. She has this idea that you might want to do the opposite, inviting the queues instead of preventing them. She thinks it through and ponders how to make the argument, considers the words, puts together sentences that sound good to her, but there's no suitable moment, she doesn't want to interrupt anyone's silent focus and so she waits, and it is in this wait that Hieu has a brilliant idea. This is on the fourth and penultimate day of berry picking. They're standing in the middle of nowhere, in open terrain: moss, a tree here and there. The swampiest marshland you could ever find. Lan Pham says something about cloudberries, that even though they're rare it would make sense to pick those too, since they're in the forest anyway. They could charge five times more for those. What she says about cloudberries is fascinating, especially the price – five times more! – but so far they've barely encountered a single cloudberry. That orange gleam is rare. From afar they look like cute little oranges, and the quantity is very limited. Cloudberries remain a dream. They plod along until they find a good spot. A blue glow. They've completed today's second relocation.

When they've put down their backpacks and fanned out, Hieu and Má and Lan Pham and Auntie Tei Tei, silently dispersing: this is when Hieu speaks up.

What if we put water in the berries?

It's just something he says. Nothing happens when he says it. Nobody responds, nobody says anything, it could be an ordinary silence, one of the many different silences that exist between them, but already from the outset this specific silence is rooted in Hieu's words about putting water in the berries. They consider it without speaking. Is that a good idea, to soak the berries in water before selling them? Má's legs are twitching. Suddenly she wants to go home and do it right away, soak the berries and let them drip off just enough, making sure you can't tell they've been tampered with by the time they're in their neat little plastic boxes on the vending table. She resolves to start as soon as they get home. One more day. It's dizzying, every time she thinks about Hieu's proposal, and she just knows: this idea of soaking the berries will be mentioned as soon there's a chance, as soon as there's time to properly consider it.

LARSMO

On Friday Má and I took the bus to Larsmo, right outside the city. Má was going to play cards with the Vietnamese at Mr Tèo's. We were going to stay for two nights. Má had told Hieu that he could call whenever he wanted.

Mr Tèo lived alone in a two-room apartment. His adult son had moved to Vaasa. The group was made up of Má, Mr Tèo, and a younger, unfamiliar woman, as well as Mr Chim, who had travelled all the way from Tampere. Xuan – Xuan with the green eyes – had stayed home with the rest of the family. The card players were playing around the clock.

I mostly holed up and read in Mr Tèo's son's old room. His books and things were still there. Football posters hung on the ceiling above the wide bed. Litmanen, Kanu, Brolin, Rivaldo. There was a TV. That evening I restlessly surfed the channels. It was the normal array – SVT, TV4, MTV3, MTV, YLE, Eurosport – but also a channel we didn't have at home, with blurry pictures in strange colours – grey and green in a strange mixture – and choppy sound. I did my best to focus, but it was impossible to follow – I switched channels several times but caught myself immediately jumping back to the one that kept showing those unusual images. Now and then a face would flash by. These were people with brilliant, green faces and their naked bodies sometimes emerged out of the grey-blurry raster. I switched channels, I switched back, there was something magnetising about them, those naked people in unusual colours, I watched them until the late into the night.

The next morning, I woke on top of the cool, fluffy duvet in Mr Tèo's son's bed. I stayed there for a long while, looking around the room. That day, in the soft afternoon light, I saw for the first time what things really looked like at Mr Tèo's. The apartment was nicely designed, different, the walls were decorated with film posters and in the doorways there were drapes made of long, hollow bamboo tubes that rattled when you walked in and out of the rooms. The living room had a shelf for films, most of them Japanese. On the wall next to the round card table, which is where the adults congregated from dusk to dawn, there was a poster of Hidetoshi Nakata frozen in action, his hair bleached, wearing AS Roma's burgundy jersey, the ball at his feet. A handsome poster, whose dark colours matched the room's furnishings, but a confusing discovery. Had the son put this here, or was Mr Tèo a football fan as well?

There was a relaxed atmosphere in the living room. Mr Tèo cooked the food himself, he made coffee for the adults and green tea for me – a weak cup, the bitterness barely noticeable – so that I could join them. A lamp hung low over the table and our faces were half in shade, half lit.

Japanese cities...

Japanese films...

Mr Tèo talked and talked, Japan was a favourite theme, but if you listened carefully you might catch a thing or two about other, regular things as well.

Larsmo was such a boring place. No traffic, no places to gather. Mr Tèo lived in one of the few high-rises in central Larsmo, where there was nothing other than a grocery store and the motorway to Kokkola and Jakobstad. I found a football down in the yard and dribbled between the currant bushes, I kept it airborne beneath the grey sky. Even the weather was boring here. I spent most of the time indoors with my textbooks. I intended to study, I was trying, but I couldn't find my focus. I flipped through the books and nothing caught my interest. I sat there as if I was waiting for something. I wanted Má to talk to me, but breaks in the game were rare. They played through the night.

During one of those rare breaks Mr Tèo made noodles for dinner. It seemed like Má was doing well, based on her wily smile and the looks she gave me when nobody was paying to attention.

I joined her at the card table.

I took a new interest in the game, learning about the different strategies and the consequences of various decisions. It was both the game itself and everything that happened around it.

At one point the unfamiliar player, the younger woman, tried to provoke Má.

Mr Tèo's compact CD player stood on the kitchen counter and ever since we arrived it had been playing music from Mr Tèo's record collection. *This*, he said, *calls for atmospheric music*. To the soundtrack of Mr Tèo's atmospheric music, the younger woman had lost three times in a row. Her complaints were loud, it was simply a question of bad luck. How was it possible, she wondered, over and over, to land such a bad hand? She wasn't a religious person but nevertheless had to ask if this was not a *punishment from God!* She reminded me of Lan Pham in Tampere, that time she'd re-entered our lives.

The others didn't say a word. The woman turned to Má. She asked how things were in her life, if everything was okay back home in Jakobstad. A polite inquiry, but the silence that followed was sombre, charged. How were things at home? Má looked at her cards.

Oh, just fine.

She had won a lot that night. It was her night. She smiled, and sometimes she convulsed as if suppressing laughter.

The stranger pressed on.

You have two sons, right?

Má stared at her cards, she was in the zone, two sons, that's right.

Because you know, I've heard things about your eldest... People say that he's no good with girls...

Má won again. She barely looked at the stranger, just smiled at the room; the cool, spacious living room with posters and shelves full of videotapes. She grabbed my arm lightly, I was sitting next to her and it was as if she did this to somehow indicate that we belonged together. The young woman looked straight at Má.

I'm sorry, but it's honestly disgusting... To attack a girl like that... I say this as the mother of a girl...

When the round was over and it was time for everyone to show their cards, the younger woman tossed hers on the table so you could barely see her hand. The others reached over the table to piece them back together. They really were bad, absolutely terrible, her cards, *heavens*, someone muttered, *what bad cards...*

From my seat next to Má at the card table I could sense that she was going to stand up and walk off. It was bound to happen sooner or later. Maybe it was the thickening cigarette smoke they were blowing at the centre of the table all night, round after round, a smoke that rose and settled within the walls of the living room. It was like an image, it made me think of something. It was as if I already knew.

Má woke me early the next morning. We were going to leave with the first bus. It was too early, but she simply left, didn't make a big deal out of it, she got up and walked out with my hand in a stiff grip. A rushed farewell. Mr Tèo sat at the card table and watched us leave. Then we heard him run down the stairs after us, we walked into the dewy morning air and hurried to the bus stop and I turned around and saw Mr Tèo in shorts and slippers, he looked sort of suspended outside the open door to the building. I watched him for a long while, I watched him until the bus came around the bend and Má pulled me along by tugging my arm sharply. We boarded the bus and she immediately whispered: she'd done really well, she'd won more than 3,000 markkaa. I felt like leaning against her, letting her close her arms around me as she sat there and whispered her joyous message, but when she'd finished whispering we both looked ahead, Má and I, each in our own seat at the back of the bus. I knew Mr Tèo was still standing on the landing, watching us. Má didn't as much as glance at him.

YES, AROUND THE NECK

On the day he was going to see the therapist, Hieu was overwhelmed by a sudden illness. He got up from the sofa and walked toward the kitchen with his empty water glass, he put a hand to his forehead and leaned against the doorway, slouching like a sack. Má asked what he was doing, and he responded in a forced voice, very low and pressurised, saying he had a headache, that maybe he should cancel his appointment. He was about to sit down right there, on the threshold, when Má gave him a long look. Her jaws tense, she asked if he was out of his mind. She pointed at our bedroom and instructed him to go lay down and rest. She would bring him tea – cancelling was out of question.

I was frozen in place on the sofa, tense and alert – as if waiting – I sought her staring eyes and finally she talked to me. She informed me that I was to accompany him. Hieu and I would go to the city, the clinic was in the centre of the town, the exact centre, in the Holländer House above the kiosk; I was to go there and sit with Hieu in the waiting room until someone came out and called his name. He would go in and talk to the therapist, and I would stay and wait, simply sit in that waiting room and wait and wait and Hieu would be in there for about an hour. I could bring a book or flip through a magazine.

Má went to our bedroom carrying a piping hot cup of jasmine tea with ginger.

He was already feeling better. Just a headache, it had faded, I didn't need to come, he was clear on that, he said so several times, and finally even Má was convinced that I didn't have to go, that it would be fine without me.

He went alone.

Time passed quickly when he was away.

Má told me that everyone at work acted as if nothing was wrong, but she knew, she could sense it, she was sure that as soon as she left the room it was all they talked about, this incident with Hieu. She told me there were other jobs she could imagine doing, jobs that required strength, jobs that required owning a car – lots of Vietnamese worked at mink farms, which was heavy labour but paid better than the laundry. She talked and talked.

Hieu came home singing so loudly that it echoed through the stairwell. He went to the bedroom and stretched out on the bed with his clothes still on, looking at the ceiling. He didn't close his eyes at all, he stayed there until Má asked us to come to the kitchen. We were going to drink tea together – she hadn't baked, she hadn't cooked, just tea, and we were going to sit together and talk.

Hieu began on his own initiative. The therapist was an older woman with grey, cropped hair. There were paintings everywhere in the room and you sat facing each other, very close. It wasn't long before Má interrupted him. She asked if the therapist was the kind who wore a shawl.

Yes, around the neck.

Má erupted in hollow laughter. She got up from the table left the kitchen, her laughter filled the entire apartment.

Shawl!

She knew it.

They're naïve... Whiteys... They think you can talk about everything...

CÁTASTRÓPHE

We made fun of Joakim in school, we'd been making fun of him all week, ever since his presentation on Euphrates and Tigris.

He'd been calm and collected in front of the blackboard. Euphrates and Tigris regularly flooded, the explained, but the ancient Mesopotamians viewed it as a blessing.

There were floods, but it wasn't a...

It wasn't a...

He looked up from his notes, his eyes on the wall at the back of the classroom. He was searching for the word...

It wasn't a...

Cátastróphe.

Cátastróphe! Someone in the front aped him but nobody laughed. The classroom was dead silent for a moment, and then he finished his presentation about how the fecund soil, made so by regular floods, enabled flourishing cultures in ancient Mesopotamia.

Later during breaktime someone commented on his strange pronunciation, and now it was obvious. We would not be able to forget this fact about Joakim.

Cátastróphe...

The result: a constant emphasis on the first syllable, the way you speak in Finnish: méchanic, cáfeteria. The joke held for a long time, it was enough to imitate Joakim to pull down loud, raucous laughter.

At breaktime, mid-period.

Phénoménon!

Rácoon!

It was a strange time. It wasn't just Joakim. That week — all week, Monday to Friday — it was as if the other students were watching me. They were talking to each other while they looked my way, and I kept getting drawn in, somehow it was unavoidable. Once during breaktime, I heard Mattias's sister gossip with her friends about what had happened. The bruises. When the girl was back in school again her classmates had been appalled, she'd looked terrible. She understood that she had to conceal the mark on her face, cover it with makeup, but she'd left the other bruises and there they were, shifting in colour for several weeks, from blue to green to yellow, then brown. Mattias's sister shared all this, her eyes big. I listened to the whole story. Then I left.

WAS SHE YOUNG?

The apartment was messy. We cleaned a lot, but everything was scattered – clothes, newspaper, photographs. Someone had left them there to be seen, on display.

One day I found a photograph of Má as a young woman.

She's holding a wine glass: fingers loosely curled around the foot of the glass, held aloft, she's toasting. She's in the centre of the picture, the light is bright but she's not squinting, there's a glow over her face and she looks right at the camera, fixing it with her gaze. Her mouth is half open – she's caught mid-sentence. There are the contours of people in motion in the foreground, everyone dressed in festive attire: white shirts, long dresses. A man's smile – his teeth, but not his eyes.

Trees and their shadows, which cast wide stripes over the festive people. Red paper lanterns hanging overhead. Má wears a long, blue dress, it's tight over her waist and arms.

The photograph was on the shelf in the living room, next to the stack of bills and government mail. I held it in my hand as I studied it carefully.

What was it?

Was she calm?

Was she young?

At night, before going to bed, I put the photograph on my desk, but the next day I found it in the living room again, on top of the circulars on the coffee table.

People in motion. The lanterns in the background, the fruit trees; the unripe rambutans hanging in thick, green bunches at the top edge of the frame. Má is in the centre of the crowd.

THE POWER OF REASON

In geography class, Veikko told us about tectonic plates, earthquakes, and floods. I was in the habit of going back over the main points at the end of the day – notes from the blackboard and things the teacher had said with more emphasis. When the final period ended my classmates burst into the hall along with all the other students. I heard them laughing and yelling out there, getting their jackets, running down the stairs, while I stayed behind, I took my time.

I read from the text. I closed my eyes and repeated the information to myself. When I was done and went out to the coatracks, everyone was gone. My jacket was the only one left. It was me and the staff: cleaners quietly shuffling past, teachers on their way to or from their lounge.

At home I kept studying like always. I sat at the desk between our beds, looking through the window onto the yard with the tree and its floating branches. Long autumn days without Hieu. There was no telling where he was. I heard Má glide over the floor in her cloth slippers. She moved slowly, she was careful not to distract me and I took advantage. I studied without interruption. Sometimes I lost my focus, but whenever I caught myself drifting away I brought myself back, as if I could use the power of reason to control my attention. I stayed in my chair and now and then I would look back over my shoulder to make sure Má was still there, barely visible and barely audible, in the kitchen or the living room, at the vanity – I'd caught a glimpse of her, always in motion, as if in flight – and then I'd rapidly redirect my gaze and straighten my back. I could not, under any circumstances, let myself be distracted... But the images returned. It was as if the two went together, keen studies and keen daydreams.

On moonlit nights I lay awake and listened to the sounds outside. I sat up and looked out at the empty, illuminated street. No traffic, no shadows. I could picture them even with my eyes open, Má and Hieu in the dark forest. They pushed in, made themselves known, these memories that were becoming my own. Why had they recurred – was it because I'd looked at those photos? As soon as I wasn't busy with something I got lost in them. The light and the sound, the insects. As if by necessity, as if by some kind of need – it was as if I had to walk alongside them, reanimate them, there was something that compelled me to drive them on, these images of Má and Lan Pham and Hieu and Auntie Tei Tei, push them farther into time, deeper inside the incomprehensible whirring of the dense, invisible swarms in the light and dark of the forest.

At first they would only show up at night, but then they came in the daytime too, when I least expected it: at the traffic lights on the way to school, at the kitchen table on a warmish, quiet day. Sometimes all I had to do was to look at something too long. Má and Hieu, Lan Pham and Auntie Tei Tei, they came and went, they were brought into being, in sharp relief in the dim landscape.

LINGONBERRY EXTRACT

On the fourth night they wash in a brook. They take their time. Lan Pham lets everyone use her shampoo. The lather shifts in pink; it's a shampoo with lingonberry extract. The foam streaks the brook. Lan Pham and Auntie Tei Tei head in different directions, one down the stream, the other one up. Má and Hieu bathe together. The brook is babbling and it's so beautiful how the stones make little hills for the water to skip across. Hieu gets out, he kicks the pine needles off his feet. He gets dressed and walks to the backpacks for a plastic bottle full of water. He drinks some. Má is wrapped in a towel and Hieu can barely see her, an indistinct shape in the middle of the brook. The water reaches past her shins; she's crouching close to the ground, squinting at the sun up high.

KUDZU

One day the final period was cancelled due to the teacher claiming to have a migraine. I went straight home after lunch. Má had aired out the apartment; it felt fresh in there, the floors were shiny, there was a scent of freshly baked cookies.

Mr Tèo was in the kitchen. His jacket was in the hall, hanging on a clothes hanger from Má's closet. Má was stirring sugar into her tea and they were talking about the weather, what the weather had been like and what kinds of weather they hoped for in the near future. There had been no thunder at all this year. They talked about mutual acquaintances, other Vietnamese people. Some who lived in Jakobstad and some who were still in Vietnam. Mr Tèo shared a childhood memory, a day he'd spent in the cornfields with his grandfather. They talked about bosses and pay.

When I entered the kitchen Mr Tèo asked me about school. I mumbled an answer. Má put a few cookies on a plate. They were round, with a dab of dark-red jam in the centre.

I heard them talk about Japan one single time. It was when Mr Tèo described the Japanese forest, how it was distinct from the Vietnamese forest... He talked about a Japanese climbing plant... *Kudzu*... Someone had brought it to the United States in the nineteen-thirties because it was able to counter erosion... But it spread like wildfire... It took over massive swaths of land, killed other plants and trees by suffocating them... It was able to swallow cars and buildings, whole cities, with those swollen tentacles... It had no natural enemy...

Má was mostly silent, but midway through Mr Tèo's exposition about this plant, kudzu, she asked if he actually knew anything about Japan, really. He opened his eyes wide. Was this a joke? Didn't she know that he knew a great many things about Japan? He leaned back in his chair.

Japanese architecture...

Japanese movies...

He even knew how to speak a bit of Japanese.

Má said that for someone who'd never set foot in the country, he talked an awful lot about Japan...

They changed the subject.

Mr Tèo and Má stayed in the kitchen all afternoon. I went to study, and just before he left, he came to stand in the doorway behind me. He said something but I barely heard him, I hadn't realised he was about to leave, I was focused on my cookies and the book on my desk, I was looking out the window. It was already evening by the time I saw Hieu cross the yard with his heavy backpack.

We ate dinner in silence. Hieu scarfed down the food and the remaining cookies in one go, in deep concentration.

What had Mr Tèo been doing at our apartment? It was as if that incident in Larsmo had never happened, as if he'd never ran after us like a dog, down the stairs and all the way to the landing without Má even giving him one look. Talking to Má now he'd used words I'd never heard before, and not Má either, because sometimes she asked what they meant. *Freelance*. These strange words from his mouth, *freelance*, *journal*, for some reason made me feel calm. I was at ease. I could tell from my breathing; that afternoon, even before he'd left, I exhaled.

GO HOME AND WRITE A POEM

Hieu was back from his second therapy appointment and Má couldn't be still. She got up and stood next to the kitchen table and Hieu started talking and Má walked back and forth, disappearing into the hall. She returned, jaws tense.

It was as if she wanted to know what Hieu had told the therapist even more than she wanted to know what he'd done to the girl. Má asked if the therapist had asked him about the bruises on the girl's arms. At this question Hieu stood up so suddenly that the legs of his chair scraped the floor. He left the kitchen without a word; the conversation was over. Afterwards I found him sneering in bed. I was in my bed, pretending to read, and I squinted to look at him. His shoulders and waist, the curve of the hip a line against the bare wall.

The hours went by. Eventually he couldn't keep it to himself anymore. He came into to the living room and unleashed his mouth. There were a few things they'd discussed during these sessions that he hadn't shared yet. For example, he revealed that after their first session the therapist had encouraged Hieu to go either to the beach or deep into a forest. This, she'd told him, might help him *calm down*. The beach or the forest. He was to stand there and look at the waves or the trees. And he had something else to share, too: during his second session the therapist had encouraged him to go home and write a poem. This thing about the poem was the final thing he said before leaving Má and me in the sofa, silent in front of the TV.

NO PAUSES

I no longer paused in my reading. That was my most important habit. I summarised entire paragraphs, I read and memorised, word for word. I told myself: if I never paused the images wouldn't come. No flickering light, no animals moving in the cool darkness.

SHADE AND BREEZE

In the middle of the night, when Hieu gets up and steps out of the car, he notices a flickering light in the trees. It's far away — at first it resembles a low, twinkling star, and he wonders if it's some kind of celestial phenomenon, a falling star maybe. When he gets closer, he realises that the light mostly sweeps the ground, in an odd, regular rhythm. At first it rests on the bushes and brambles, then it darts over the tree crowns. He walks closer, away from the car.

It's Auntie Tei Tei.

When he sees her out there, the only light in all this darkness, he realises that Auntie Tei Tei must not have slept a wink all these nights. That's why they've picked so many berries in such short time, a feat that's amazed both Má and Lan Pham.

Auntie Tei Tei freezes when she hears Hieu. She turns, the light from the headlamp following her movements, and she looks straight at him, fixing him with her gaze.

Hieu's mind is racing, he thinks about tomorrow when he'll tell Má, he'll do it first thing, he'll tell her under the dewy firs, explain that Auntie Tei Tei hasn't slept at all, not a wink. He imagines Má's reaction, the way her hand will fly to her mouth, he thinks that no matter how she reacts his revelation will shape the entire day, the whole drive home. Auntie Tei Tei hasn't slept, he'll tell her, *not a wink*, and the moment Má hears the words she'll have to accept that this is absolutely, completely true. This is the truth: Auntie Tei Tei really hasn't slept a wink since they got here.

Hieu is about to return, he's managed to slink out, he's on his way to the car when there's a beam of light in his field of vision, a total surprise. Auntie Tei Tei's headlight follows him, illuminating his back in the cool dark of the night. He finds the car and quietly opens the side door. The cargo area is stuffy. He hears the soft breathing of Má and Lan Pham – he can't see them, but he hears them. When he turns on the flashlight that hangs from the ceiling he jolts at the scene: they look so innocent, Má and Lan Pham. Deep in sleep, dressed in thick hoodies and scarves wrapped around their necks. They whimper at the light, shift, then keep sleeping. Hieu gets in between them – there's a lot of space in the centre of the floor – he turns off the light, pulls the covers over his face, and pictures a leopard moving over a bare slope.

It is a leopard that wanders through the darkness, into the dense forest. It lays down in the shade of a lonely pine – warm and thick like a velvet curtain – and falls asleep. Waking up, it rests its eyes on the hazy tree crowns down below.

It is a leopard that stands, then walks back to the copse, the dark yet clear copse. It was an open garden in the daytime before darkness chased the heat, making way for shade and breeze. The cool, sharp darkness that already speaks of the morning's arrival.

It is a leopard, it stretches on its long back legs. Yellow eyes. Vertical, motionless pupils.

Moss falls apart under its heavy paws.

It is a leopard that walks up to the watering hole.

Underwater, rinsing off the blood: a strange, muffled soundscape, rocks slowly knocking against each other.

Dripping, golden-brown fur. Dark spots. All that's left is the leopard's colours.

The animal walks back to the dead bodies, still warm. A doe and her calf in the moonlight. It is a leopard that tears into the flesh, chewing blindly. Swarms of newly hatched insects. The tracks of blood alluring: wide and wet.

It is a leopard that keeps him awake. He's aware that a sleepless night is to be expected, it's not the first time. Sometimes it's not even worth trying and maybe he should just do what he tends to do in situations like these: close his eyes and wait for nothing, stay in the hollow nighttime darkness. But there's something unusual about this night. Auntie Tei Tei is out there, and he can't help but think of the darting light, it's already getting into his eyes, flashing under his eyelids even when he closes them, even in the darkness underneath his comforter. He listens to Má and Lan Pham sleep, listens to the empty space between the inhalation and the exhalation. Nothing happens in that space: he pictures it as steady, heavy sleep. He listens carefully, making sure, and that's when he decides to sneak out again, for the second time this night.

Tonight he can't stay in place, tonight a magnetic longing propels him. He cautiously opens the side door. The pail is with him, an insurance of sorts: he plans to hold it with both hands, making sure it's visible, in his meeting with Auntie Tei Tei.

THE PICTURES OF LAURA

Whenever I stood in front of the closed door to our bedroom – a door painted in a pale shade that took on a shiny, silvery colour when the sun touched it – I saw straight through it. The wood was transparent, it revealed the image: Hieu's back, slightly rounded, bent over Laura. Her trembling arms, the fingers that swept the vertebrae of his back, that grabbed his shoulder blades, pulled at them, wanted to open him up.

The pictures of Laura with us on the beach. The sea stretched out in front of us like an oily mirror. We ran until we were tired and played a strange game where everyone except Má crawled on all fours over the cool sand, moving slowly like turtles. Eventually Má was crawling, too. Muffled laughter. The waves polishing the rocks.

A self-portrait: close-up of Laura's face, head-on: a glimpse of the white arms that hold the camera, a wreath of red wisps of hair, freckles. Eyes closed, cracked lips forming a smile.

On the pedestrian street, at the inauguration ceremony for the new fountain. An MC at the microphone, facing the crowd on the cobblestones surrounding the structure. Children screaming, intermittent glints of sun. Laura... Laura in the crowd, far away. A grey shawl covers her red hair. She brought her bike to the edge of the pavement, still far away, her animated face in the haze, the shifting reds of her hair: orange, coral, dappled and sparkling with gold, almost yellow. Then, in the shade: almond, rust brown. Her green eyes in the shade. Laura was there...

Hieu was at the front edge of the crowd, close to the MC, and I was by his side. We were surrounded by his friends, a bunch of them, and all around there were families, children, retirees. Hieu was talking to two ladies, he had them wrapped around his finger. He looked them in the eye, talked about the fountain, expounded on how much he liked it. He turned around and appraised it, from the bottom up. An oblong, oddly shaped metal construction. One of the ladies laughed bashfully, rubbed something off her cheek, covered her face with her hand, and Hieu just kept going. It was a good name, he felt: *Yhtyvät virrat / Streams Coming Together*. She was toast, this lady, you could see it in her eyes, the way it moved from his mouth to his eyes, from his eyes to his mouth.

Laura, still far away: suddenly panicked, both hands on the handlebars of her bike, her arms close to the body. Looking at us. And then, her eyes darting all over the place. She looked away from the crowd. She walked the bike off the pavement and then got on it with surprising nimbleness, sort of kicking and flapping, before she sped off towards Rådhusgatan in her yellow dress.

BLUE FINGERS

Má interrogated Hieu as usual after his third therapy session. He'd barely walked through the door, hadn't even hung up his clothes, when Má pounced with her questions. Hieu told her that he'd read the poem he wrote, said it went well, said he'd left the paper with the poem on it for the therapist so that she could read it again if she wanted to.

Má was now working on weekdays. The boss would call her whenever someone didn't show up and needed to be replaced that day. These were busy times for everyone.

When Hieu said that he'd shared his poem with the therapist it was as if Má realised she'd made a devastating mistake. She opened her eyes wide and covered her face with her hands. It was as if she'd broken the law.

Incomprehensible.

A poem...

Was she worried, was she scared?

She could have calmly processed this fact – Hieu had written a poem – but instead she was in despair.

A fiasco.

How *could* she have forgotten?

Hieu had been asked to write a poem.

She'd known this for a week.

Hieu was unable to say what the therapist had done with his poem. Maybe she'd tossed it, maybe she'd brought it home with her. Má asked if he could remember anything from the poem, *the actual words*, and Hieu replied that of course he did, but he didn't feel like sharing. He couldn't remember the whole poem and this meant, he argued, that it was better to refrain altogether.

Má had forgotten that Hieu had been asked to write a poem. We would never speak of this disastrous event again, but I often thought about it. I imagined Hieu writing.

Hieu: paging through his textbooks, looking for words.

How did he go about it?

One day I came across a ballpoint pen among his papers on the desk. I saw the bitemarks.

He had chewed on the pen.

Blue fingers.

I imagined his fingers, stained by ink, in the fluorescent light of the school library, where he sat in an armchair, gaze pinned to his notebook. Legs crossed. He was serene. An immeasurable, incredible calm. He found himself feeling a new kind of loneliness, his thoughts were unreachable.

I pictured Hieu with the pen in his mouth.

Blue fingers.

An end to his doubts.

A JOYOUS DAY

Má was preparing for a phone meeting. She walked back and forth, in and out of the hall, dressed in a blouse and skirt. At the appointed hour she sat down on the stool next to the phone. She watched it until it rang.

'Yes, yes'; 'good, good.'

A brief conversation. She put the receiver down and leaped up, she took me in her arms, she walked into our bedroom where Hieu was doing push-ups, bare-chested in the middle of the floor, she interrupted him with a joyous yelp before embracing him and dashing out of the room, pinching my cheek as she went, back to the hall and the table, where she grabbed the phone and excitedly punched in a number. When the person on the other end picked up she wheezed into the receiver.

I... got... it...

It was a day of joy. We went to the kiosk, Hieu and I flanking her, we stayed close together while walking through the cool shade of the tree-lined streets to buy chips and lemonade. She got it. They had called from Jakobstad Daily. All of their regular photographers were otherwise committed or home sick. The manager had reached out to his substitutes, Mr Tèo among them, who told him that unfortunately he was unavailable that day, but they should try calling Má.

Not a single photographer in the entire town available. An unlikely situation.

He'd given them her number.

Fäboda had a new horse stable, where everyone was welcome. She was to photograph the horses.

WHAT DO YOU DO WITH A HORSE

Má was so focused on photography that you could enter the room and she didn't know until you were right next to her.

Horses in their stalls, horses under the sky. She hadn't asked the newspaper person what kinds of photos they wanted. She claimed that doing so might have *jeopardised her chance*. She turned to Hieu with a wily smile and asked if he might want to head over to the stable in question and look around, ask a few questions about their activities. He scoffed and replied that she'd said we'd all go there together. Apparently, Má's proposal was just crazy.

What do you do with a horse...

She took pictures of the furniture and she took pictures, through the window, of the kids playing in the yard.

IN ONE SCENE

Má told us about a dream she'd had multiple times that week. In this dream we'd moved back to Vietnam, all of us, she and Hieu and I, as well as Lan Pham and Auntie Tei Tei, even Gunnel was there amidst the palms and plum trees. *In one scene*, Má said, Gunnel was at a street kitchen, dressed in a loose dress, about to pay for her *bánh bao*!

She described other events from this dream. Certain events she spoke of as *scenes*.

MINOLTA 35MM SLR

Where do you end and where does the camera begin?

With a Minolta 35mm SLR it's almost too easy to capture the world around you, or express the world within. It feels comfortable in your hands. Your fingers fall into place naturally.

Everything works so smoothly that the camera becomes a part of you. You'll never have to take your eye from the viewfinder to make adjustments.

Minolta lets you concentrate on creating the image instead… You're free to probe the limits of your imagination.

MINOLTA
When you are the camera, and the camera is you

SÖREN BÄCK

Saturday was the day. We went with Má to the stable. The location was all wrong, on the other side of town, way outside the centre, halfway to Fäboda's sandy beaches. We walked for a long time on a winding country road – gravel, meadows, little woods – until we arrived at a dirt field with horses. Má took out her camera.

Black dirt, woods.

Three black horses were standing around a haybale in the centre of the pen. They chewed lifelessly while looking at the ground.

Click, click. Má took a picture. Hieu and I were standing on either side of her.

Somewhere a car door slammed shut with a dull sound. A man in black, square-frame glasses emerged from the low-hanging branches near the side of the road. He was walking in our direction. Má kept photographing the horses, she was looking into the viewfinder, she had one eye closed, it wasn't until the bespectacled man was standing by her side that she looked up.

'Sören Bäck, hello. I'm a sports journalist.'

They shook hands.

Sören Bäck opened the gate and walked into the pen, past the horses, without looking around.

There was the proprietor, Judith. Hose in hand, she was in the middle of cleaning the stable floors, she was almost done, she apologised and said that a lot of muck collected every day. Sören and Má, side by side: Sören with his notebook, Má with her camera, and Judith jogging across the floor in her tall boots. She got two plastic chairs and she and Sören sat down, facing each other; they began the interview. Sören asked his questions and Judith answered right there, in the centre of the floor amid squat bags and shelves full of helmets. Belts and whips hung from hooks on the wall and there were unusual tools everywhere. Haybales in the corners, shovels and pails. Sören asked about Judith's background and her new business.

We walked over to the horses, who hadn't left the haybale. We stood there for a long time, at what you might call a safe distance. The horses were chomping sluggishly while they gazed out at the empty fields. Hieu asked if Má shouldn't go closer. She was there to photograph the horses, after all, not the trees or the sky.

When the interview was done Judith thanked us all for coming. She said it was too bad that we'd come so early. Today was an open house for kids, she told us, lots of fun activities, but it was usually busier in the afternoon.

I looked at Sören Bäck and his hunched back as he returned to his car.

I looked around.

The horses out there...

The bales of hay...

Judith and her strange implements...

It was hard to imagine what any of it had to do with sports.

Má could stay as long as she wanted. Until she had what she needed, Judith said. We approached the three black horses. Hieu and I were shivering in our hoodies. Brief glances. Click. Click. Má got onto her tiptoes, camera in her hands above her head. She crouched.

She complained.

Nothing looked good.

The biggest horse sauntered off toward the road, its head softly swaying, and we pursued.

Má took many pictures. Hieu was standing right by her side: suddenly focused, as if ready for something. Má was about to get a new roll of film from her handbag and Hieu put his hands out. He had custody of the camera for a moment and directed it at the horse, as if to take a photo. Má opened the film packaging. Hieu said something about the light and she nodded.

The gleaming fur of the horse in the morning light, the swelling muscles and their chiselled, blue-shimmering contours. The horse had put its head over the fence, the mane blowing in the wind.

I looked at Má, who looked at Hieu. He said something about *the composition*. He advised her to go stand at another angle, and she nodded.

Má and Hieu and I and the horses. No matter where you looked everything was muddy and grey. When the first visitors appeared – a mother with several children in a red car – we were finally getting ready to leave. Judith ran up and put her arms around Má who thanked her, and then we departed. Hieu took the lead. I looked at him, his buoyant steps, as he walked at the head of our procession.

Má was going to the newspaper offices with her film rolls tomorrow already.

The composition...

It was her first job as a photographer and Hieu had given her advice.

AFTERMATH

The last photo of Laura. Laura and Hieu napping on the other side of the room. Their arms hanging over the edge of the bed. It's some kind of aftermath. The plastic flower on the windowsill. Bright, but no sun.

A FRAME IN A MOVIE

I left the apartment and walked towards the town centre. It was Sunday and most places were closed. I went to the library. The memory of Hieu's advice to Má – use a different angle to improve the photo's *composition* – burned bright in my mind as I entered and sat down among the bespectacled old men and women in the reading room. They were all busy with the papers, and so was I. It didn't take long for my mind to drift off. Tellushallen, Besnik and Juri; teammates. I saw them in my mind's eye, I heard their laughter echo against the concrete walls. Floodlights, everyone looking, the high from a pass that cut through the defence.

I would resist it all.

Autumnal sun through the tall library windows.

A football magazine ranked the best players in the Veikkaus League. I read the magazine until I got hungry and walked home across the empty square. Rectangular candy wrappers lay like fat snakes on the pavement. I couldn't stop thinking about Hieu's words to Má at the horse pen. *A frame in a movie...*

He'd offered her lots of advice that day. She didn't react to most of it, but at one point he'd said something that stopped her in her tracks. It was outside the pen and right after we'd said goodbye – Judith had thanked us for coming and now she was returning to the stables – that's when he'd said it, no big deal, spontaneously, as if it was something he'd thought of right there and then.

When you take a photo... Think of it as a frame in a movie.

Initially it didn't seem like Má had heard him, but then it was as if it was sinking in, as if Hieu had said something incredible, something she'd never thought of before. She let go of the camera and let it hang from her neck. Then she took his head between her hands and kissed his forehead. She held him like that, their foreheads touching each other. She looked into his eyes and he looked back. We'd said our goodbyes, we were about to leave, but now we were stalled, he'd said that thing about a frame in a movie and Má's eyes were shiny. I looked at the barren fields. A frame in a movie... What terrible advice... Wasn't that the first thing that came to mind anyway, to think of the photo as a frame in a movie?

Any day now, Má's photographs would be printed. Mr Tèo subscribed to the paper and had promised to call as soon as he saw the reportage about Judith and her horses.

The frame in a movie...

A comment made in passing, as if it was something he'd just thought of.

Why should Má listen to Hieu?

He never watched movies.

He didn't care.

He didn't even know how to act around girls.

Má had a dream, and I was bound to it.

She walked around the apartment with her hands clenched in fists. Mr Tèo could call at any moment. She got the box that was full of documents and photographs.

Blurry self-portraits.

A photo of Hieu and me in the hall, his hand on my shoulder.

Hieu already had a new girlfriend.

Nature photos.

Bushes.

White tree crowns. Crow tracks in the snow.

Did he sleep at her house?

The flowerbeds in Runeberg Park.

Rock formations.

Nighttime photographs. The eyes of a cat.

Blurry, incomprehensible photos.

She needed to practice.

Má had a dream and I could help her.

When she got dressed to go out I did the same. She was standing in front of the hall mirror with the camera around her neck and I stood next to her. Half of me was visible in the reflection. We took a long walk, all the way to the industrial area, to the papermill and the shipyard, we continued to Vestersundsby and then toward the town centre, we walked home via Skutnäs and the fancy little houses. I knew that she would walk slower if I walked slower; I knew I could make her stop this way. I slowed my pace gradually leading up to a crosswalk, and then we paused at the intersection; she took her camera and pointed it where I pointed my gaze, as if I was leading her.

A red car in an empty car park.

Crows.

Two boys, one older and one younger, hand in hand, by the traffic lights.

I had to know what was beautiful.

For something to look beautiful, it doesn't have to look exceptional, she'd said, but it has to be positioned *right in the picture*.

We paused, then hurried on. Má's attention was caught by the strangest things. At one point she crouched, resting an elbow on her knee, very focused, to photograph an empty can in a ditch. Another time she went to stand right next to a stop sign.

We turned off at the intersection following the wooden houses in Skutnäs. There was a pizza restaurant and a bar at the intersection, but prior to these businesses, in one of the high rises shooting up from the pavement... That's where Lan Pham lived. We were on Lan Pham's street. All of a sudden we were in a hurry; I sped up, rushing down Lan Pham's street without looking around, I knew Má was right behind me, that we'd take the quickest route home – without stopping, without saying a word.

A few weeks later Má got the pictures from that day back from the developer. Wide shots of Jakobstad's streets. Skies and clouds. The red car in the car park. The crows. The pictures followed one another, a predictable order. I'd already seen the boys at the traffic light. The empty can in the ditch, the stop sign. I thumbed through the photos, feeling breezy, until I got to the last twelve in the stack. I counted them later on, the twelve photos at the bottom of the pile, photos that would remind me that we'd found ourselves on Lan Pham's street that day, that I had sped up with Má in tow. My memory was clear: we'd found ourselves, as if by accident, on Lan Pham's street, we'd hurried down her street until we got to the roundabout and turned onto Skutnäsgatan. It was a clear memory that did not correspond to what was in front of me – the photographs told me that Má had hung back.

First, pictures taken from the street: Lan Pham's kitchen window. Blurry, sloppy photos, taken in haste.

Then: pictures taken in Lan Pham's yard. She had entered the yard of Lan Pham's building.

A photo of me, by the swings. I had gone with her. I'm smiling at the camera. Zoomed-in pictures of Lan Pham's balcony. The plants, gone to seed, drooping through the railing. Wilted, darkened flowers.

I was sweating as I flipped through these pictures. I looked at myself, leaning against the swings, and it really was me: green windbreaker, looking at the camera. A smile.

What was this?

I tried to interpret the pictures, hoping to find something in them.

Did I look pitiful?

We took that long walk together, Má and I, and I was there to help her.

Was I *sweet*?

I looked at myself and then I saw it: I was absolutely clueless, I looked like a clown. There I was, in the yard of Lan Pham's building, below her window, posing! Má had tricked me up…

I had to keep moving through the stack. Before I was done looking at the photos I had the thought that sooner or later Lan Pham would appear in one of them. Standing at the window, the outline of her face, her eyes wide-open behind a sheer curtain. I was beside myself, I stared at each and every one of those twelve pictures and Lan Pham was nowhere to be found.

HE WAS WAITING FOR THE CAR

Hieu had written a poem, which Má, thanks to her forgetfulness, never got to see. Hieu had read his poem to the therapist. He'd torn the page from his notebook and given it to her. When Má heard this she brought her hands to her face. She would never know what kind of poem he had written.

What was this poem he had written?

Hieu had never studied, he had never truly studied, he had never studied with dedication and focus.

I had.

I knew that Má knew it: I was the chosen one.

It was to me that the images came.

It was I who was haunted by the events, and I had the sense to turn away from them.

In contrast to Hieu.

He was a good-for-nothing who barely made it through school.

He'd punched a girl.

He bragged about me in front of the older students at breaktime, said I was good at football. He protected me against Má's slaps and he took the blame when I'd forgotten to lock the bike and it was stolen.

He had a new girlfriend – there were already rumours about it, whispers in the schoolyard.

He didn't know how to get good grades.

He fell in love with Isabella with the round cheeks.

He fell in love with Laura and they were so in love.

He'd punched that girl from school.

He had a new girlfriend.

The therapist had asked him how things were at home, how things were in school, how things were with Laura. That was something she did — asked three questions at once. It must have been a quiet day. I pictured him looking at the floor between the therapist's feet, as if he was waiting for the car, and when the car drove by outside, he replied that it was over with Laura, that he was the one who'd left her after all.

NO TEXT

I never had reason to go that way, but one day I biked the length of the street that intersected with ours, all the way to the cul-de-sac by the squat industrial buildings. The sturdy metal doors to the laundry were visible from the road. There was a hint of the cloying, sharp scent of rose, lavender, and lemon. The corrugated metal walls had no windows, there was no way to look inside, but I knew that the inside was teeming with Vietnamese people.

Back home I went to sit by the living room window, like I always did. Mr Tèo didn't call that day either. The last evening bus came past the bend; in the dusk it looked like a ghost car. No lights, no driver.

I was alone.

It was impossible to study.

I hadn't seen Má or Hieu all day.

I thought about the horses by the haybale. Their long, pretty manes underneath the grey sky.

What was taking so long?

Was Sören Bäck slacking at the job?

Did he have some kind of problem?

I knew where he lived. I could call him. If I plucked up my courage I could introduce myself by first and last name and he would remember Má immediately. I already knew what to say, I would yell straight into his dirty ear: Use the pictures! – just the pictures, no text, no interview, just the pictures of the horses!

Every time the phone rang I thought it was Mr Tèo calling about the pictures. Or Lan Pham. As soon as the pictures were published we'd be able to move on. Finally, once and for all. We would leave the blueberries behind, the movies and the laundry. We would be in uncharted territory.

SNEAKING

I pictured him with the pail in hand, sneaking farther and farther away from the car.

CICADAS

The headlamp hasn't left his pocket. He's used to the darkness now. He stops to fix his socks, which have slipped down inside his rubber boots, and it's when he bends down to pull them up that he first hears the sounds. They're coming from far away. Some bird. Wind in the trees: a soft, regular whooshing that makes him think about ocean waves. He walks deeper into the forest, sweeping through the terrain that expands before him like an invisible bed of crackling brambles and bushes. Every now and then he pauses, trying to figure out where Auntie Tei Tei is, but the sounds are the same every time. Some bird, and the wind.

The night is strikingly quiet, still. He reaches for his headlamp anyway, attaching it to the elastic band, which he wraps around his head. It's like magic: the light follows when he moves his head. He turns off the lamp to rest his eyes. He turns it on and off. The light makes him dizzy. He takes it off, but immediately changes his mind, tacking it back on. A new attempt. Swaths of the landscape, illuminated. The sharp light makes the dark-green pine needles look like they're billowing. The buzzing of invisible bees. He feels the humidity against his face, the sweat on his lower back, inside his arms. Other sounds. Cicadas.

Cicadas?

Frogs?

He can see them now, the lianas that bind the trees to each other.

He speeds up, goes deeper. He's careless. Pictures the ant hills, reptilians sleeping belly up, monkeys resting in the trees, snakes. A mother snake with her baby snakes, seeking shelter for the night. He finds Auntie Tei Tei at last, a hazy glow between the tree trunks, a flickering between the crowded branches. He's pulled in her direction, moves unencumbered, hovering over the brambly terrain. As he gets closer she looks his way with one hand covering her eyes.

Please, that light...

It's the first time she addresses him directly. He looks down, then up at the sky, trying not to blind her. And it's while he's doing this, his head moving this way, then that, tilting up, tilting down, that he hears the sound of water. A distinct sound, as if from some unimaginable place. It makes him think of waves breaking against the shore, of sea birds.

He looks down, then up. Finally he turns off the light. He stays put, and Auntie Tei Tei comes toward him. She walks slowly. Twigs break under her feet. He feels her breath on his forehead. She touches his head with her hands. His lamp comes on and she's blinded, she squints. Then it softens. Hazy, pale – Auntie Tei Tei has dimmed his headlight. She takes his hand and starts walking and he follows even when she drops his hand, as if he's being pulled along by a line. His head movements are now accompanied by a soft light. He's moving fast, he's attentive, he can't lose sight of Auntie Tei Tei.

They arrive at a gently babbling brook. The forest is dense all around, nobody can see them standing there side by side, Hieu and Auntie Tei Tei, waiting and listening with their headlamps directed at the darkly purpled water.

Hieu closes his eyes.

Auntie Tei Tei stays by his side; he hears her shift on the soft, spongy ground, moving her weight from one foot to the other.

He shuts his eyes, and a moment later there's a new sound, different from the brook, a sound from up the hill, and it's coming closer. Paws. Leaves, twigs, and pine needles break under the slow approach. Swishing, crackling sounds – this is clearly a heavy animal.

When Hieu finally opens his eyes he sees something speed off. He's able to catch a glimpse: an elongated shape, the size of a moped. Some kind of cat with tasselled ears, apparently panicked and disappearing into the underbrush. Spotted fur.

Auntie Tei Tei has gone into the water. She's seen it all, that much is clear when you look at her, the way she leans forward with her hands underwater and her neck extended, like she's ready to pounce, facing the slope where the cat was resting only recently.

Hieu is tired.

He feels ready to do anything.

He feels ready to lay down in the water.

He's sweating.

He imagines the muddy bottom against his bare feet.

He shuts his eyes.

Cat eyes in the dark.

The city's darkened streets – even the windows are black. He pictures the cat eyes on the flowering, tree-lined street.

Blurry spots.

He sees the feline cross the yard.

He puts a hand out and Auntie Tei Tei takes it.

Sweaty night.

He gets into the brook, his hand in hers.

They bathe in the warm water.

He opens his eyes.

He washes the dirt from his face.

Bright glow.

He sees the berries. He sees Auntie Tei Tei's face emerge from the water…

He sees her mouth, but not her eyes.

He walks up to her in the water.

He hears her wild laughter.

She's laughing.

He's laughing, bright and easy, he hears their laughter echo high in the tree crowns, he uses his laughter to conjure the images.

He sees Má soak the berries in water.

He sees her weigh them, in the kitchen, it's a morning so bright it's blinding.

He sees them at the market, their swollen berries, Auntie Tei Tei and the cousins, Lan Pham, Gunnel and her husband. He pictures himself talking to the customers, he pictures the parents of his classmates coming to say hello. They embrace like friends. He pictures Má's Vietnamese acquaintances: watchful, skulking at the end of the queue.

He pictures Má next to him, wearing a white blouse. Her hair is wrapped in a silk scarf.

Sheer clouds move as if pulled by threads across the low sky.

He pictures Isabella in a floral dress.

Isabella and her mum; Isabella's mum at the stand asking, isn't that Hieu, Isabella's classmate, did he help pick all these blueberries?

He looks at Isabella's thin, white arms.

Soft, pink sun.

He feels ready to do anything.

He feels ready to lie down on the asphalt.

AT PEACE

Hieu is reposing in Auntie Tei Tei's arms. When he opens his eyes the two of them are looking in opposite directions. She's regarding the trees, and he's gazing past the top of the hill, where the berry bushes droop over the slope in fat bunches. He shuts his eyes again. He drifts in and out of sleep. The back of his head is comfortable against Auntie Tei Tei's bosom, he's tucked in, neck muscles gleaming in the moonlight. He wears his hoodie like a wimple. Auntie Tei Tei is caressing his forehead, the bangs that come out of the hoodie, her hand moving slowly, like a painter's brush.

She bends her neck so that her head comes close to his; their noses touch, he's breathing softly, he smiles and she smiles, and he turns and she looks up at the trees.

He inhales to fill his lungs.

He's absolutely, completely serene.

At peace.

He's right here, in this moment.

Birds' wing strokes echo over the swimming hole, a shallow pond filled with mud and rocks. Grey, cloudy water that reflect the low clouds.

They haven't slept all night.

They bathe again, they return to land. Moss crackles underfoot.

Sun.

They stand, backs facing each other, naked in the sunlight that sifts through the branches, and she begins to speak, her voice hollow like a robot's.

There was a summer I spent in Saigon, the streets were sticky, I was outside the hotels, in the alleys, there was a soft film of bloom over everything... A terrible time, humid heat all over the country, your mother had cut her hair off... She wasn't fragile... But her needs were quite specific...

FINNISH ZOOLOGY

They are about to embark on their journey home. Everything glows in the dewy morning. What a time they've had. Hieu sits in the middle and he keeps looking at the pails in the cargo area, they take up almost the entire space back there. Má drives slowly. It's as if her mind is elsewhere. Auntie Tei Tei says something about a *leopard* and Lan Pham flinches, she can't believe it, she looks around in distress, she inhales as if to say something but remains silent, heavy breathing. It's the last morning. They've all let their gazes linger on the bushes, the leaves, the tree trunks and the flowers, the stalks and the leaves. And up close: the bees and the ants in their anthills. They've even paid their respect to the mosquitoes, let them suck the blood from their arms one last time before they leave. Má changes the channel on the radio and the volume shoots up. Hieu smiles, enjoying the music, until Lan Pham turns it down so low that you can barely hear the singing. There's just the bassline and the drums and the gravel smattering against the car's metal.

Later on: a lively discussion about Finnish zoology. Auntie Tei Tei has made the same comment in passing several days in a row now, claiming to have seen a leopard. On the drive home the car is silent, they're halfway there, and suddenly Lan Pham brings it up again. She requests their attention. There are no leopards in Finland, so Auntie

Tei Tei has not seen a leopard, and that's the end of that. It's crystal clear, she notes, very easy to grasp.

On the day prior to market day Má soaks the blueberries, twigs and leaves removed, in water. She puts the buckets in the shower one by one, making circles with the showerhead, its gentle, bent stream.

When the day comes they're gathered on the square, beneath the parasol, their expectations sky-high. Everyone is there. Auntie Tei Tei. Lan Pham. Gunnel, who swings by before work to wish them luck. Lots of customers comment on the price: it's not cheap, but it's 'a good price'. Hieu reveals himself as a sales talent. He serves the customers from behind the table, striking up conversation even before they address him. Tells them about the berry-picking, doesn't even blink. A nice harvest. A nice spring, a nice summer. Sweet berries. He moves his hand in a sweeping gesture over the berries, touching them, showing off. The day is warm. The sun burns bright. Now and then a cool breeze pulls through the square; Má takes note of it each time, this breeze. It's never cool enough, she thinks from her spot under the parasol. She looks at the berries, looks at the way they gleam, almost shimmering, as if they'd planned it all along: only the berries would be in the sun. She lifts her gaze and checks their surroundings. Hieu really is a star at this. He hooks the customers, reels them in, sells kilogram upon kilogram. Things are unfolding so smoothly that Má never has to worry. She's able to let her thoughts stray.

Kids chase each other between the market stands. Hot dogs and cotton candy. The air is sweet and sticky. People take a rest on the stone steps under the court house's rounded arches. Má looks at the clock on the building's tower, its sharp spire. Flagpoles jut out at an angle from the second-floor balcony, and the Finnish flag flutters in the breeze. It's a never-ending afternoon. The cashbox is getting heavier and heavier, but they still have several hours before they can go home and count the money. And it is in this empty space in time, in this wait, that a young man shows up with a plastic box in hand. He's been by before, a handsome, polished man. Hieu remembers. They talked about the weather and the man bought three boxes; now he's here again, under the parasol, jutting up against their table. He's all up in Hieu's business, fixing him with his gaze. This man gestures with the berry basket, he squeezes it with his hand until there's a cracking noise and juice trickles down the plastic inside walls. He says he's been cheated, and Hieu immediately, as if by reflex, reaches for something under the table. He maintains eye contact with this man, a stranger, and asks, in a friendly voice, if he'd like to buy bulk instead, but when he puts the heavy scale on the table the man leans in and grabs his arm. He grabs Hieu's arm and demands his money back.

Má has allowed her attention to drift out over the square. So many people. She studies their faces. Pale and mealy, even though it's already afternoon. There's the sky, with the rippling Finnish flag. She notices the cloud, there it is, one single cloud, grainy, barely a cloud anymore. This disintegrating, flattened cloud: for a moment she allows her gaze to rest on it, her face turned toward the sky, and Lan Pham and Auntie Tei Tei glance her way.

This thing she is doing right now, it's not like her.

She's not doing what she's supposed to do, she's distracted.

In this oddly quiet moment, when Má is looking at the sky, everyone, even the stranger, seems to be holding their breath in anticipation of her reaction. There he is, with Hieu's arm in his hand, but nothing happens...

When Má finally, at long last, turns her attention to the events unfolding before her — when she sees it, Hieu's arm, right in front of her, when she sees how it's gone white at the most narrow part, the protruding bone of the wrist, and when she realises that this man, a stranger, is standing right there, his hand around Hieu's arm — when she realises this she takes a few steps forward and here everything happens as if in one single motion, as if choreographed — she takes a few steps with her finger pointed at the man's face, she comes very close to him — the nail, painted red, is right next to his eye as she roars three words in Vietnamese. It's a real scream, you can hear it tearing at her throat. The three ugliest words in Vietnamese, and she screams them at the face of this stranger.

Lan Pham can barely control her own laughter. They're in this tense, frozen standoff, everyone all serious, everyone is looking at the man, this stranger, waiting to see what he will do next, this man, who's purchased berries at an inflated price — and Lan Pham is about to burst into laughter. An odd reaction, inappropriate, even, but the thing Má just said... It's so ugly...

What is Auntie Tei Tei doing? Her eyes are closed.

Auntie Tei Tei has shut her eyes in shock.

Má hands the man, this stranger, two plastic baskets, which is as much as can fit in her hands, half a kilo of blueberries, which she is clearly offering as a gift, and when he seems uninterested in this gift she makes him take it. She forces him to accept the gift, it happens fast, she opens his hand and he accepts, he stops staring at Hieu, he turns around and storms off, not even a glance over his shoulder, not even once, and finally he turns the corner with his baskets, he's out of sight, they're alone again.

They exhale.

What an ordeal.

And what luck, Má thinks, that he gave in so fast. She had the sense to act, she proved herself quick-witted, but now she knows that this was only the first of many complaints. She watered the berries too much, they're too heavy, anyone can see it.

What was she thinking?

She glances Lan Pham's way, Lan Pham is looking out for clients, bouncing on her tiptoes, it looks as if she's trying to bend her gaze down the street to spot the hordes that must be on their way to mob the square. Any moment now. She's so clueless, Má thinks, and a person like that, someone so naïve and clueless, that's not someone you can share your dreams with. These are her thoughts as she agonises under the midday sun; she catches herself in the act of coming up with new, mean descriptions of Lan Pham. Lan Pham – her only girlfriend! – who's helped her in so many ways!

Later on, a young boy approaches their table and now Má is all keyed up. She's all keyed up and then she's relieved, exhales, when he turns away. She's thinking about the weather, she finds herself hoping for rain. She would like a wild, whirling rain to sweep in over the square, to get underneath the parasol and on the berries, a wild, protracted rain, and she knows that this is but an empty wish – not even a real hope – because the forecasts all promise sun. A round, beaming sun, 20 degrees all afternoon.

VIETNAMESE PEOPLE EVERYWHERE

The days went by, uneventful. Moments of waiting contracted and all at once the sky had closed around the final rays of greenish autumn sun. Má was bustling in the kitchen. The table was set for two, her and me. Music came in from the yard through a little crack in the window. White cabbage, fish sauce. A comical hunger: she giggled, I gobbled down the food.

The phone rang. She stood up with care, and then left the kitchen, moving slowly so as to finish chewing. She picked up the receiver; then she frowned. Something was going on. Maybe it was just someone whose Swedish was too difficult. She just stood there, a grin on her face. I got up and joined her in the hall, moving like she had: slowly, chewing. She handed me the receiver and I said hello, said my name. A woman, speaking in Finnish. A friendly voice. She spoke so slowly that I could hardly believe it, every syllable extended. It was Laura's mum. She said that Hieu had come by again, that he'd been standing outside, late at night, and directed a flashlight at Laura's window. 'Taskulamppu', a flashlight. She said they'd call the police if he didn't stop.

Má had time to take a long shower before Hieu came home. He came home and she said nothing, her lips were smooth and soft. He hung up his jacket and then she began to hit him, first with an open hand across the face, and then, when he was kneeling against the wall in the hallway, she took the shaft of the duster and struck again and again, rapid blows over his bare arms, she was yelling at him when he was on the ground.

A long night. It was only when his breathing was deep

and regular across the room that I could picture it with any real clarity. Hieu, under Laura's window, the wind blowing, semi-hidden by cattails, unmoving in the darkness, ready with his flashlight. I rolled to the other side, squeezed my eyes shut, and sleep came. In my dream, Hieu and Má are walking down an empty, foggy street. It's a rapidly dawning, cloudless night. Plastic tables and chairs chained up on empty patios. Mopeds, sleeping dogs. Flowers wet with dew hang over balcony railings, glimmering like fish scales. It's morning by the time they arrive at the bus stop, and when the bus rolls up the people queue to get on. It's a spacious bus. The country road leads to the coast through a series of small, hazy villages; they make a stop for food, parking behind a truck. Hieu and Má disembark with the other passengers, they take a seat on the plastic chairs on the terrace, eating and drinking in the shade. A fishing village: when they gaze over the roofs, they can almost see the sea. They pay their check and move, excited, down the narrow, airless alleyways of the village. A smell of offcuts and urine. They arrive at an open port. A market on the quay, fresh-caught fish and silk shawls. The sun lights up their sweaty faces. They wade out and Hieu bends down, putting his hand in the water. He then brings that same hand – his left hand – up toward the sun in a triumphant gesture, letting a few drops of the salty water land on his dry, pouting lips. He walks to where it gets deep, dips his head in the water, holds his breath and emerges with a big smile. He turns and looks back at the street, watching the palm trees against the strange colour of the sky. Then they keep moving, following the stretch of beach to the orchard that rises out of the sand. They're standing in the shade of a straw roof and a young man offers them a plate of watermelon that's been cut into boats. It melts in the mouth. Má spits her seeds on the ground in front of Hieu and their feet are matte from sand and dust, their legs too, all the way up to the knees. Then they return to the beach, running, chasing the children to the sound of their wild laughter. Má and Hieu, both of them tireless. First they run, and then they walk the perimeter of the bay. It's a long walk, they move slowly, they look at what the waves have brought to the shore: plastic bags, shards of glass. They walk back into the water, wading, and they stand in the light of the red sun so that their hair burns and turns as brown and yellow as the sand. They look at the water, Má with an amused expression, she's looking at her own reflection and tosses her hair so that it smacks her shoulder blades. Hieu looks at the translucent jellyfish that float around his legs, he's entranced... Until Má tells him they're poisonous and he scampers out of the water... He's smiling but his body is twisting as if in rage, the waterdrops cascade around him, hissing as they land in the white sand. Má turns to him, flinging her yellow hair back. Laughing, she scoops up a jellyfish with her bare hands, balancing it between her extended arms so that it slips from one wrist to the other and then into the water. Hieu: tense, ready. He's in the sand, he's looking at the fishing boats which look like they're turning into vapor in the hot sun. Then, without warning, he sprints back into the water. For a moment they stand side by side, the waves lapping the sand between them. He shuts his eyes and wades out farther, he walks with his eyes closed, the soft lapping of the water comes above his waist. Má looks at him, squinting, smiling. She's underneath the palms, the plum trees. Vietnamese people everywhere. Red sun, pink sky.

BIOGRAPHIES

Quynh Tran (b. 1989) grew up in Jakobstad in Finnish Ostrobothnia and now resides in Malmö. A graduate of the acclaimed Biskops Arnö Writing School, Tran's debut novel *Shade and Breeze* was awarded the prestigious Runeberg Prize, the Svenska Yle's Literature Prize, and the Borås Tidning's Debutant Prize.

Kira Josefsson is a writer, editor, and translator working between Swedish and English. Her translations have been shortlisted for the International Booker Prize and the Bernard Shaw Prize. She lives in Queens, New York, and writes on U.S. events and politics in the Swedish press.

SHADE AND BREEZE
Copyright © Quynh Tran, 2021
Translation copyright © Kira Josefsson, 2024
First published by Norstedts, Sweden, in 2021.
Published by agreement with Norstedts Agency

This English-language edition first published in the
United Kingdom by Lolli Editions in 2024

The right of Quynh Tran to be identified as the author of
this work has been asserted in accordance with Section 77
of the Copyright, Designs and Patents Act 1988

SHADE AND BREEZE is No. 18 in the series
New Scandinavian Literature

Graphic design by Orin Bristow
Typefaces: Alte Haas Grotesk, Fournier MT
Printed and bound by TJ Books, Cornwall, 2024

All rights reserved. Except for brief passages quoted in
a newspaper, magazine, radio, television, or website
review, no part of this book may be reproduced in any
form or by any means, electronic or mechanical, including
photocopying and recording, or by any information storage
and retrieval system, without permission in writing from
the Publisher.

The cost of this translation was defrayed by a subsidy from
the Swedish Arts Council, gratefully acknowledged.

SWEDISH
ARTSCOUNCIL

A CIP catalogue record for this book is available from the British Library

ISBN 978-1-915267-28-3

Lolli Editions
New Wing Exchange
Somerset House
Strand
London WC2R 1LA
United Kingdom
www.lollieditions.com